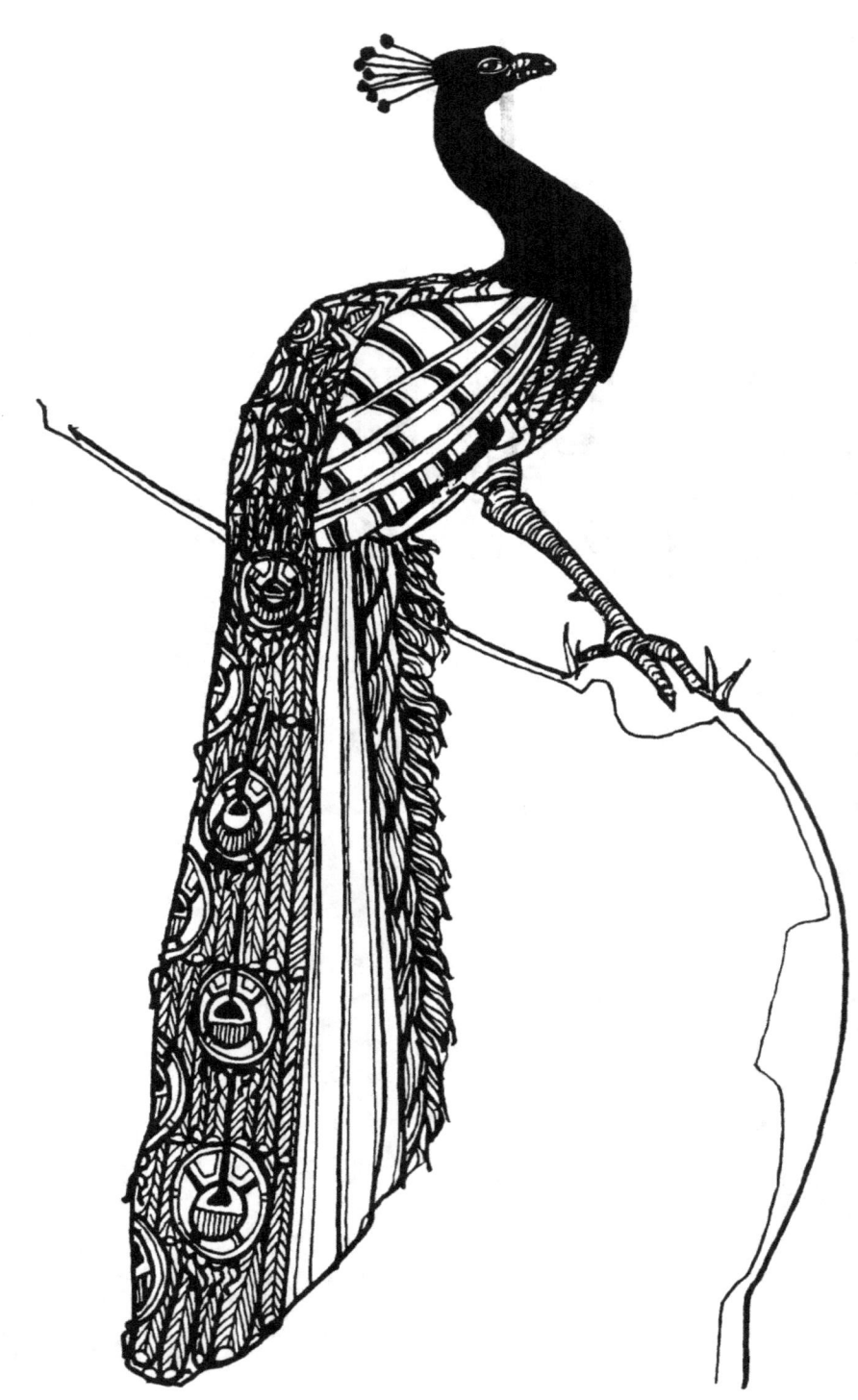

PULP Literature

PULP LITERATURE PRESS
Issue No. 15, Summer 2017

PULP *Literature*

Pulp Literature Press, Publisher

Jennifer Landels, Managing Editor

Melanie Anastasiou, Acquisitions Editor

Janet Eastwood, Assistant Editor, Acquisitions

Katherine Howard, Wendy Christensen, Assistant Editors

Daniel Cowper, Poetry Editor

Amanda Bidnall, Copy Editor

Mary Rykov, Proofreader

Kris Sayer, Graphic Designer

Rachel Kuo, Advertising Co-ordinator

Susan Pieters, Consulting Editor

Cover painting *The Huntress*, by S Ross Browne. Illustrations for 'Gruff' by Kris Sayer. Illustrations for *Allaigna's Song: Aria* by JM Landels. All other illustrations by Mel Anastasiou.

Pulp Literature: ISSN 2292-2164 (Print), ISSN 2292-2172 (Online), Issue No. 15, Summer 2017.

Published quarterly by Pulp Literature Press, 8540 Elsmore Road, Richmond BC, Canada V7C 2A1, pulpliterature.com at $15.00 per copy. Annual subscription $50.00 in Canada, $66.00 continental USA, $82.00 elsewhere. Printed in Victoria BC, Canada by First Choice Books / Victoria Bindery. Copyright © 2017 Pulp Literature Press.

Pulp Literature Press gratefully acknowledges the support of the Canada Council for the Arts.

Canada Council   Conseil des arts
for the Arts   du Canada

Pulp Literature is a proud member of the Magazine Association of BC.

TABLE OF CONTENTS

FROM THE PULP LIT PULPIT

Sensual Summer Reading

There are seasons to reading, and summertime reading brings a wide smile to the face of avid readers. It's not just the stories publishers print this time of year, selected to delight and intrigue, but the addition of excellent and necessary props that go along summer reading.

The furniture turned so that sunlight hits the pages straight on. Something cold in a tall glass, so we don't have to stop reading too often to refill it. A chair that, like well-designed shoes, settles the reader comfortably backwards. Furniture with arms that invite us to loop up a knee, or a padded settee in which we can turn upside down, feet overtop the back rest. Gravity makes it harder to sip while reading, but easier to smile.

The book could be any book. For some it's an old favourite to be swept across with eyes and mind, like flights of crows scanning Middle Earth. It may be an epub, easy on the wrists and eye, or crisp new pages straight from the shelf, or a thick-leafed novel from the past. *Arrowsmith* in black and gold. *Forever Amber,* printed, for some reason, with a green cover.

And the time to read. Long days, warm nights, trips to the library in flip-flops with a big cloth bag.

However you take your summer reading, we hope and trust you'll love this issue. We'd be grateful it if you'd let us know you like it. We'll answer you in a few minutes — we just want to finish the next few pages.

Cheers!
Jen & Mel

GOOD BOOKS
for the price of a beer
Short stories, poetry, and comics you can't put down.

PULP *Literature*
pulpliterature.com

*I*N THIS ISSUE

Iconoclasts and troublemakers run amok in this issue.

A young vagabond risks her soul against magical forces to save a world that's been anything but kind to her in the opening chapter of **Brenda Carre**'s novel *Gret*; and Spencer Stevens encounters a rebel heiress in his search for his own lost love in 'The Highwayman's Deception', Book Four of the Seven Swans mysteries by **Mel Anastasiou**.

Aliens, dragons, and trolls are not what you might expect in **A M Soto**'s 'Pack Up Your Troubles', **Charity Tahmaseb**'s 'A Knight at the Royal Arms', and **Kris Sayer**'s 'Gruff'.

Chill out by the pool in two Californian tales. Murder and sexting go hand in hand in **Adam Golub**'s 'The Pool Guy', and 'Cannery Row' by **Susan Pieters** is a bittersweet coming of age tale.

Our poetry editor Dan Cowper has selected three brilliant works for this issue. In **Benjamin Hertwig**'s 'Inglewood Courts, Edmonton', a young Croatian ventures into strange territory;

Nicholas Christian's 'Wassail in Ink' leaves us guessing at seven words; and **Jenny Blackford** startles with 'The Hair in the Bag'.

Short and sweet with a sting: this issue holds the Bumblebee Flash Fiction contest winner 'Crushed Velvet', a comic tale of rebellious clothing by **Ingrid Jendrzejewski**; and runner-up 'Kiss Kiss Bang Bang', **Jay Allisan**'s glimpse into a utopian yet all-too-familiar future.

You may relax, but these characters cannot: a hurt and hungry man takes centre stage in **Angela Post**'s 'Sourdough', the Surrey International Writers' Conference Storyteller's Award runner-up; and **JM Landels**'s Allaigna wields swords and magic in her search for her father in the latest instalment from Book Two of the fantasy trilogy.

GRET

Brenda Carre

Brenda Carre *writes long and short fiction with a dark, mythic twist — stories often set in locations near her home on Vancouver Island or in the Chronicles of Ardebrin, the epic fantasy series she is currently crafting. Brenda's short fiction has appeared in* The Magazine of Fantasy and Science Fiction, *as well as anthologies from Fiction River and Ragnarok Press. We are delighted to publish 'Gret', the first chapter of her forthcoming novel of the same name, a preview of which also appeared in the acclaimed* Blackguards Blacklist: Anthology *(Ragnarok, 2015). 'The Clunkety', also featuring Gret, will appear this fall in the* Superpowers Anthology *(Fiction River). More about Gret-the-witch, Ardebrin, and Brenda's art can be found at brendacarre.com.*

$\mathcal{G}$RET

My mam always told me there's three ways to prosper best and all begin with L.

Location's one. No prospering's ever done by thief or witch if the job begins in the wrong place or time. Lissom tongue is next. No matter how much wisdom a gal has to her, good learning don't go far if she can't talk her way out of a bad deal. And last is Lightning Touch. That means the effortless sliding of nimble fingers in and out of pockets without bein' cotched.

My mam knew these L's right better than any I've met. She could charm the gold (and other things) right out of any feller's britches. We'd a Red Lamp and Physic House just outside the palace gates of the Grand Corsair of Roon. Back then us Red Lamp girls was good for much more than pleasure to bodies in need. We were spies, healers, and counsellors. We had the ear of high folks on Roon. And witchery. Mam passed hers on to me. No brag, just fact. She could fix the dying so they might live again. She could deal with those what needed killing. She called it her laying-on-of-hands.

My da was one who lived and loved, so she said. Word was

he'd been a Corsair, like so many were on Roon in my younger day, his gull-grey Xebec as swift and trim as any true seaman's craft could be. I guess I got his beak of a nose and his uncompromising temper. Handsome, mebbe. I can't say. 'Easy on the eye' got him nowhere in the end. My da was hanged after a fierce battle in a little town called Skyhaven upon the rugged Isle of Inach. Hanged from their Raiders Gate along with the rest of his crew. The villagers torched his ship, the fools. No good sense of true thievery among the lot of 'em.

Rank, lubberly fisher folk. Heads so far up their arses they needed to shout to be heard.

Don't guess Mam grieved at his loss. Not for long. She was a cool witch. For her it was business first and womanhood second. Most like, I'd be just like her, save for my 'nuncle Vongy.

The day Mam died, that sodding bag of dead man's piss knocked me over my tender young pate and threw me into the orlop of a pirate ship. I'd just turned thirteen.

So there I was, cotched and away out there on blue water.

Now, that was a real bad location. No silver-tongued happiness was gonna save my cherry. A little maid no more, I'd begun on the road to the witch I am.

Isk, the captain, was no true Corsair. Pirates ain't. Pirates'll rut with a post if there ain't no goats aboard, and the goats breathe easy if there's girls. Old Isk was a barnacle-bottomed fiend with a snout like a dead salmon. His breath smelled like toenail slime. His frowsty periwig was so greasy even lice wouldn't live on it. His hands were never still.

He didn't bother to untie my hands. Keeping me bound got him randy. He'd a preference for young flesh and he had it often. He made it clear to his crew I was his property, bought and paid for with his coin (leastways 'til we got to the mainland and he could get a better trade for me).

I took his using of me and I festered with hate. Pretended I liked it. I used that lissom tongue my mama had taught me, trying not to vomit in the doing. Knew well enough to wait my time 'til we made Trinceport.

That first night we came ashore, just beyond the oil and tar smell of the Trinceport ship-yards, on our way to our louse-rid bed in the attic of some noisy ale-house, we passed a stinking midden. It lay beside the hulking fish-gutting house.

To my delight I spied some fungi growing near. A clutch of White Hoods! I knew 'em well. I managed to trip and fall flat on my face, my bound hands flailing, and snaffled one into my rags without Isk seeing me.

How I longed for a decent time to dry them proper (more pain in the dose), but given my hasty need, I took the ghostly cap and sprinkled the spores into Isk's claret. He drank deep, got randy. I did what come un-natural.

Later that night, when them White Hoods took effect, when that bugger was unable to do more than whimper, I thumbed out his eyeballs and fed them to him. I didn't bother with his tiny balls. Without his eyes, his sailing days were over.

I grabbed Isk's meat knife and a bannock or two for my tattered pockets and I was out that windee and into the shore mist faster than a clam can fart.

Farther up the hill above the scum-shacks of Trince lie the palaces and the high houses of the merchant guild. I didn't dare go there, though I was hungry; I'd heard enough from Traders in Roon to know that was folly. Those buggers have dogs that can chew the skin off your face.

I ran out-town instead, warming up some as I ran. (I refused to take that bugger's cloak with his smell and his rot inside.) I stole some eggs and some windfall apples from a fisher-folk steading and got as far away as I could before anyone knew what I'd done to Isk.

I lost (and I do mean lost) myself deep in coast dunes with a nail-paring of a moon lighting my way and then the black-night hulks of trees so old they were standing even when them infernal *Kahin* lived in these lands. Back then there were some places where the trees were tall as mountains. No undergrope 'neath them monsters. I expected bears, or pards, or even restless ghouls, but nothing on our Goddess-green soil was gonna make me stay where Isk's crew might find me.

At first, that forest could'a been aflame from the rage in my heart. I cussed the dark, I cussed old Vongy, and I cussed whatever might try and git me before I got a chance to settle my score with that arse. I et my apples and my bannocks and I cussed myself sick.

By then, my chest hurt bad. Felt like the Gods was carving me empty with a trowel. Fact was, I wasn't sure I'd followed Mam's advice and picked a good location. I'd no silver, no map, and no true direction, and prob'ly no straight way of getting on any boat back to Roon wouldn't sink like a boulder in a gentle swell.

I limped bare-footed over the cold, damp ground and the night come for me, into my heart and into my soul. I spewed out everything I'd et into a pile of tree needles and I went on. Empty and done withal. My innards went to hatred, cold and icy and sure.

Could'a put my heart in a sling and used it for shot.

That's when I started to cuss the Goddess. "It's *you* what

brought me here, damn ya, and I hate you, ya hear?" I hissed. Mist snorted from my nose-holes, quivering like ghosts before my night-sharp eyes. "We did naught but do your will, Leete. Both me and Mam. We was always true to ya with yer share of the silver we took. Now, how do ya pay me back?"

I shuddered with the force of my hate. Around me the air went cold as the vaults of the Spirit Kingdoms. Around me the screams of death. A stoat at a hare. A vixen screaming like a demon spirit. The snort of something huge.

Bear? Boar? I hunkered and froze. I clutched my puny knife tighter.

Then I heard something strange.

A clanking noise.

My ears pricked. I knew the sound of good coin hitting metal. If any music could'a woke me up that was it. Luck was, it scared whate'er had been snuffling towards me. That thing give a 'whoof' and bolted off, crashing away though the brush like a hut on legs.

"Fook!" breathed a voice not far off. Desperate. Young and skinny, I guessed, more by his voice than his form. A Red Lamp gal gets used to telling lots about folks without seeing 'em.

The clanking resumed. I crept soft and stealthy over the spongy ground.

It was black out as Garani's bowels, but I went careful. Breathed slow and soft. Got closer to the clinking noise, peeked over the lip of ground made by a termungous tree-root.

"Fook!" he sighed again. He was less than five strides away and working hard at something on the ground by his knees. Was he a-running like me?

"He'll kill me. He'll bloody kill me," he moaned.

His terror hit me like a fist. He searched blind at the ground, looking little more than a flailing hump in the dark. Then he began to keen. "No. Please. No! Pleeese."

Stupid arse!

My fingers relaxed a little on my knife and I got careless. Something crackled beneath me. I heard a gasp. The back of my neck fair prickled. I stayed as still as a salted codfish, but it did me no good.

"I know you're there, girl," he said.

Whatever had been there in his weakness were gone. The voice of him didn't sound the same neither. It rattled like bones and stung me with a Power as old as the stars.

"I smell you, little witch, both blood and will. I am minded to take you as one of my own, one of my dark *Azghillin*," he said. "Come out now, and it's well. Try to hide, and I'll take your soul."

Oh, Gods. What in Hells is an Azghillin?

I cringed as something out of my ken hit me. He was gonna take my soul anyways. I might not be able to read minds like Clan do (thank all the gods), but the witch in me knows the sound of a lie.

"Be light," come the smooth command.

Light bloomed under the trees so the young thief glowed like bog fire. He was mebbe sixteen or so — could see a throat apple on him that told me his nuts had dropped.

His black duds spoke of his trade. Coal-dusk hair in long braids, high cheeks, with up-tilted lids spoke to me of his people. Native Clan. A sack spilling coin lay on the ground just at his knee and spoke of his problem. I saw the hole in the stitchings what caused the spill, and a glint of a silver tube just poking out. He'd been into a hoard of some kind.

But it wasn't him had conjured up the blue light around him. He was took over. By a ghoul or demon mebbe, or even something worse. His eyes were rolled back in trance so only his white eyeballs showed.

"Drop that knife and come here," he said, staring at me with them terrible eyes.

My guts crept inside me like spiders. Power gripped me. I stood. I dropped Isk's knife. My feet disobeyed my will and walked me towards him. I wanted to scream out a warding cantrip, but my lips were like corpse lips. This was no demon nor ghoul. This was Rogue Magic.

Sorcery.

"Ah, Gret," he said. "You are so like your mother."

I gawped even as my gullet closed. Garani's black tits! This Rogue knew my mam. Even now his voice tweaked the strings of my memory harp. I remembered a tall, grey-eyed Trader who'd come to our House when I was wee enough to dandle. He'd a load of silver with him too. He'd been nothing like any other of our patrons. Quiet, aye, and oh, so polite, but boiling beneath with something so wild I couldn't bear to look at him straight.

Mam had shut the door between me and her and him, but even so, I scarpered down beneath the table's cloth and shook like a jelly until he left.

The Rogue gestured to the ground just before him. "Sit there. Face me. I would look inside your mind."

I sat. I obeyed like a fettered hound. By Gods, I'd of rolled and begged if he'd wanted me to. An invisible hand gripped me by the face and held me so I couldn't look away.

"Choose to serve me as your mother did; or choose not, and die," he told me, like he was discussing the weather.

Mam would never serve a Rogue!

I wanted to cuss him aloud, but my lips were clamped.

No? The thought come fast to my mind. *Think on her success, and on her death.*

You killed my mam, and the babe she had inside her. I didn't care I was touching minds with a Rogue, I was that bloody mad.

The Goddess killed them. Not I. She will brook no rival in me.

I snarled. Even with a bound muzzle I could still do that. I shut off my mind with all the rage I could summon.

The boy-lips moved again. "You are strong. Your hatred tells me you believe what I say. You disowned your Goddess tonight. I saw that memory still hot inside your head. You have broken your ties with Her. Your uncle Vongy belonged to the Goddess, my dear, not me. He's Her pawn but I can make him *your* pawn, Gret. Make him squirm like the louse he is, before you crush him."

His words teased me. Aye they did. I could almost feel Vongy's neck in my grip. If I'd only guessed his mind before Mam died, I'd of slit his pipes first and fed his vulture's gizzard to the Grand Corsair's wildcats.

"You are so much stronger than this craven boy," said the Rogue.

The boy's form wavered, became that of Vongy. Sly, greedy, mean, soulless bastard. This felt like no lie to the witch I am. It felt like a true Seeing. With a purr of satisfaction Vongy reached out and grabbed one of the coins from the ground. "All mine now, dear Lady," he whispered with a sleethy sneer. "I thank you for showing me which of her poisons to use on my sister."

Oh Gods.

My hands trembled.

He deserves everything you do to him, my dear. Choose my path and you will prosper. All I ask is that you aid me to put Her down. Among those coins before you lies a silver Scroll. Within it lie the seeds of my Betrayer's undoing . . .

His anger hurt so deep inside me it had no fathom. The semblance of Vongy vanished and became the thief-boy once more, and of a sudden the pressure at my face relaxed.

"What'd the Goddess do to you?" I said aloud at last. I stayed where I was. It could be folly I was listening to this Rogue, yet I felt his anguish.

"She took me from the Stars and made me love her. So long ago, it's folly to count the years. She took my magic to her own, became a Goddess with my Powers. She stole from me, and worked to destroy me."

"You want revenge, like I do on Vongy," I said. That this being — whatever he was — was a Rogue, I did not doubt. Yet he spoke Truth. I felt it in my bones. He'd been done ill, like me.

"I want justice, Gret. I am old. Older than a dragon with his fires out. Revenge is such a petty word for my last and deepest need. This fickle Goddess has thwarted the Stars, and the Stars do not forget. I am of the Stars — a Star lord. I had the power to move Suns and Moons, but now, I am diminished. Body after body I have taken over the centuries, forever on the watch for those like you to serve me. Will you join my band of young assassins? You would surely be one of the best. Will you be one of my *Azghillin?*"

"This boy's an assassin?" I replied.

My wits were at war now.

"A useless one and a worse thief." The Star lord made a noise of disgust. "These coins upon the ground, this precious item. He has lost himself in this forest like the fool he is. If you join me, Gret, I advise you to take the sleeve knife he bears and kill him. He will only hinder you."

I looked at the full sack of coin. I didn't guess it counted anywhere near to what I'd lost in Roon, but it'd be a start. "Kin I have what's in this sack?" I asked.

He nodded. "All but the Scroll. That comes to me. But more, I will give you Power. You are strong, little witch. You have great will. I do not doubt you can be taught to conjure and to cast, once you have learned from me. Are you with me? Speak swiftly. It is dark and this failed assassin tires."

"And Vongy's mine?"

He grinned like a wolf and extended his hand to me. "I can teach you to take him to pieces and throw him to the Rift Demons."

I stared at his open palm and sighed at such promise. To be able to cast a soul into the Rift of Shadow? Great Gods! Now that was Power! Even the sensuous fingers of comely men have never held such power in my hottest passion. It wasn't a boy's hand I'd be taking. I'd be taking the hand of a God, or something as close to one as made no never mind.

The failed assassin set there like a post. I could kill him. He was useless. The witching part of me that sniffs out foulness told me he was already lost. His soul had been took by Garani a long time ago. Moreover he was a coward. I'd heard that in his whining earlier. I didn't shrink from the thought of being an assassin. Moreover I hungered after revenge on Vongy and I sniffed that silver. There's dark in me.

"You gotta loose me if ya want my hand," I said.

"Be freed," he replied. "Come here, Gret."

And I did, though this was no command, I leaned forward with full intent to seize his hand and do his will.

Yet, right in the midst of my move I remembered one last thing my mam had told me.

The worst location ya can ever git in is a place betwixt the Gods in a battle. Naught but Garani's own mischief can come of such folly. If ya find yerself in such doings, drop everything, git out, and don't stop running.

Now here was me, doing just that.

I didn't seize the hand held out. With Lightning touch, I grabbed that Scroll-tube instead. It was hard as a club and it did just fine. I ironed that boy's pate so hard he went down like a butchered ox. The bog-fire went out of him and I knew in the dark I'd kilt him.

Smelt it too. Wet brains.

By Gods, this round is yours, came a last wisp of thought as that Star lord lost his grip on my mind. Then nothing. Into me come a great freedom and I set there thinking until first dawn.

It was a grey day, but a good one.

I snaffled them coins and the Scroll I'd gonked the assassin with and wrapped them all back up in the sack (well tied) and, remembering the earlier suggestion, I found the assassin's little sleeve knife in its soft leathern wrist-sheath. Sharp as a bodkin it were. Its hilt was yellowed bone. I knew enough about saw boning to tell that bone had been culled from a human arm. I strapped that unholy thing around my own wrist and stuck Isk's blade into my new *Azghillin* boots (too big, but my feet were still growing).

I turned the dead assassin on his side, fumbled about his corpse in the half-light, and found a welcome pouch tucked between his back and his cloak. As I'd hoped, there was food in it (hazelnuts, dried fruit, oats, and jerked beef) and a decent water skin at his belt. I snaffled his dark cloak and hood. Hells, he didn't need them anymore, did he? The rest I left and turned him back on his face. Though he didn't deserve such, I whispered a cantrip over him to keep the ghosts away and the ravens from pecking out his lights. More to save the souls of any who might stumble across his bones than for his dark shade.

By then, the sun was rising. Felt new warm upon me. Now I knew where East was. It was time to git.

I spent that whole day hiking uphill through wilds and thinking. That damned Scroll weighed heavy in the sack at my shoulder. As long as I had that thing, that Star lord would find me. Knew it even worse as I come to a cliff from which I could stare down on the valley of the Great River. I watched a warren of coneys jumping about like they'd not a care in the sky. Lucky coneys.

Before me the whole of the South Dales spread out around the great fan of the River. Felt like anybody could find me up there — or I could find them. I was my own witch now and that's how I wanted to stay. Nobody's fool but my own.

Below me splashed a falls. I could feel it through the rocks beneath me. I set on my hunkers and dug out them nuts and munched. Tugged that Scroll-tube from my sack. It was a rich and sparky thing, ancient gravings along its sides, something a-rustle within that smelled of musty magic. That it held something potent I sensed. I didn't look within. Didn't want to. Didn't need whatever curse lay in that thing to foul up *my* three L's.

That it would fetch me decent silver, I knew — maybe even a trip back to Roon and Vongy — if I sold it to the Merchant Guild. But that way, soon or late, it would git to that Star lord. He'd follow the path of trade back to me, and I wanted that link broken. He was more than I wanted, both then and now. See, I knew a bad deal when I smelled it.

I et from my store, set a snare, caught a coney. Knew I'd not go hungry that night. I stood at last and faced the drop before me. "I don't want this, I tell ya," I called to the air. "I don't want you and I don't want Her. Ya hear me?"

Thought I heard laughter on the wind.

"Well, fine!" I cried. "You laugh at me, Star lord. I don't care. I'm my own witch. I ain't yours and I ain't Hers. Here's at ya!"

I took that thing and I heaved it, as far as I could, up and out. It flashed in the air, turning and turning, till it fell into sound and deep. I heard it clink on the rock, and then a far splash.

I sighed. Now it was out of my ken and carried by water. Beyond the touch of sorcery. I hoped. "Find that," I told him.

Laughter answered me. I laughed back.

FEATURE INTERVIEW

Brenda Carre

Pulp Literature: *Did you create the flawed and admirable character Gret deliberately, or did she walk out of the woods into your heart?*

Brenda Carre: Gret-the-Witch strode into *Truth-Seer*, the epic fantasy novel I am currently revising. In *Truth-Seer* she is older and crustier. I loved her instantly and knew she had a back-story I was going to write some day. When Ragnarok Publications put out its open call for stories I took the opportunity to begin Gret's story. As soon as I was one or two pages in, I knew I wanted to handle Gret's life in a series of chapters that would eventually become a novel.

PL: *As an artist, as well as a writer and speaker, how does your art inform your writing?*

BC: I see so many parallels between the canvas and structure of visual arts and story. One informs the other. Both are narratives that spring from the artist's desire. Both begin with impulse, extend into vision, and finish with process. I see both as a kind of push and pull between the artist and the creation, where artist/storyteller is the vehicle for the creation, structuring it and reining it in, but always with a respect for what is being formed. The best writers and artists are those who can perfectly bridge the gap between themselves and their viewer/reader with the creation itself, which perfectly expresses the understanding on both sides, both viewer and creator. Hard to do but always simple and clear to behold.

PL: *You give brilliant workshops on world building. What was your first new world?*

BC: My first written universe was the world of the Chronicles of Ardebrin, the alternate world in which both my current work *Truth-Seer* and *Gret* take place. I began this world when I was seventeen, though I began to invent worlds long before I learned to write by lying in bed and telling myself stories. I latched onto the oral tradition of storytelling from my dad, who used to sit and tell us stories every night. I think he got his skill at storytelling from his dad, who used to do the same thing.

PL: *You live in such a beautiful part of the world. Does your own setting greatly influence your fictional settings?*

BC: Absolutely and all of the time. Many of my short stories take place here on Vancouver Island. I am currently writing a faery story, 'Ondine', for a story bundle coming out in May. It's set in New York City and on Chesterman Beach near Tofino.

PL: *Can you remember your first magical influences?*

BC: These had to be the stories my dad made up on the spur of the moment. He had a creative impulse that was deeply sensitive to myth and magic. I was lucky.

PL: *We love your use of language and special idiom. Where do your voices come from?*

BC: I have to listen hard, but if I do, I hear them clearly. Then I take dictation. Sometimes doing this is harder than others, obviously. The hardness for me is letting go of what I think needs to happen. Listening for the story voice started early on in my writing career when I began to 'interview' my characters. It freaked me out at first, because often their voices would come through loud and clear. The thought of 'voices' in your head and all that. Nevertheless I decided there was nothing alien about this after talking to other writers, and I started asking my characters questions off the cuff to see what they'd say. I always knew it was getting good when my characters would start to ask me questions back.

PL: *What projects lie ahead for you? What shall we watch for on brendacarre.com?*

BC: I'm hoping to put up more interviews from fellow artists and authors about their sources of inspiration as well as more free stories of the month. I want to return to my art and show more of that as well, once I have finished the revisions of *Truth-Seer*. I have a lot of stories that have been previously sold to anthologies that need covers and a home as e-publications. The business end of this job is at times bewildering: there are covers to design, branding to consider, and connections to make out there in the form of story bundles and shared worlds. I have several projects to write for in these areas and some revisions to make on my website.

THE SEVEN SWANS: THE HIGHWAYMAN'S DECEPTION

Mel Anastasiou

How far will Spencer Stevens, then and now, go to win back his long-lost love? Beleaguered, kind, flawed, and untalented at DIY, Spencer is an unlikely hero. In this newest adventure, forty years, five thousand miles, and a couple of marriages separate him from Holly. But it seems the Seven Swans Pub will stop at nothing to send him into perilous times and hone him into a hero who will brave a second chance at finding happiness.

THE SEVEN SWANS, BOOK 4: THE HIGHWAYMAN'S DECEPTION

CHAPTER ONE

When it comes to fixing up a terrible old building on the side of a canal, I'm the last man on earth to brag of any kind of do-it-yourself ability. A Canadian expat since the age of twenty, I've lived in London ever since. And in London, there was no do-it-yourself. For example, if you could afford a garden, which I never could, you employed a gardener. If you want an update in your loo design, you call a fellow in to shift the pipes around and knock out the plaster and then eagerly paid somebody else to put the plaster back in the walls after it.

But there are a few things in this good old world that absolutely anybody can do. Dab paint on dirty brick is one of them. So, I stood on the canal side of the derelict Seven Swans, where my handiwork was most likely to be enjoyed by passing narrow boats. A herd of friendly hanging baskets from Wilko clustered about my feet, I dabbed at the plastered brick and felt myself master of my demesne.

As the dirt disappeared beneath my brushwork, I fancied myself alone, but an intake of breath from behind me proved me wrong. I turned and greeted Stan, the aging angel who had agreed to come out of retirement to help me fix up the place.

His pal Eustace turned his head atop his skinny neck to and fro in a sorrowful *no*. "You can't do that, old son. Not and keep to the law."

There's always somebody who wants to tell a man his dreams are impossible.

I gave Eustace that business-like rictus that passes for a smile from a man heavily occupied with important affairs and kept dabbing. Eustace, I reminded myself, never seemed to know much of anything. He was more of an agree-er. Stan was the man with the knowledge. I took Stan's silence for approbation.

Then Stan spoke. "Where did you get that paint?"

"Wilko," I said. "Their best line," I lied.

"Ah." Stan nodded. "Well, you'd best scrub it off then."

"You might return that paint," Eustace said. "But your paintbrush was soiled touching the wall, so there's some dirt in it, isn't there?"

"Indeed." Stan stared glumly into the paint can.

I gazed from one old fellow to the other. It was clearly a case of two men standing about a building project and predicting negative outcomes. Not unusual in the UK. To be expected, in fact.

"It'll be all right, I'm sure," I said politely. "I'm just freshening the place up. Cheap and cheerful, isn't that what you say here?"

"Oh, yes," Stan answered.

Eustace added, "But this building is Tudor."

"From Tudor times, in fact," Stan clarified. "From the time of Good Queen Bess."

I remembered her. My princess, when I lived the dream of a labourer and solved a mystery that saved her lovely life. "That's why I'm freshening it." It was almost the truth. "In her honour."

"I'm sure she'd like it," Stan said, "as would Her Majesty nowadays. But the fact is that this building is listed."

I dipped my paintbrush into the middle of the pot. Outdoor acrylic, middle range low gloss. A classic Victorian cream. Not shiny. Tasteful and understated. It would look well with the petunias in their hanging baskets. I said, "Listed, eh? To the right or to the left?"

"Ooh, cheeky," Eustace observed.

"He's young," Stan said. I was sixty, but in the midday sun, with a paintbrush in my hand, rebelling against the advice of those older than I was, I felt young.

"My nephew would bend your ear on this very subject." Eustace sucked his upper lip.

"Let's keep nephews out of this," I begged.

Stan said, "Look, put down that brush and give us your ear before you incur the wrath of the law."

The wrath of the law! For touching up a bit of wall on a sunny day? Nothing more licit in the world of DIY, I thought. But I was building up a thirst. I opened the cold chest I'd bought along with the paint and pulled out a fizzy water for each of us. I handed them round.

Eustace took a sip and made a face. "It's not Guinness, is it?"

"I'm afraid not."

Stan took a long slug of fizzy water and belched silently behind his fist. "Look, for a listed building you can't be daubing any old muck around. It has to be paint from Tudor times."

"How am I supposed to get Tudor paint?" I sat myself in the grass near the canal. "Take the Tardis back five hundred years?"

Eustace chuckled. "I wonder what they'd make of you back then? Burn you at the stake, most likely."

"Be that as it may." Stan pointed his finger at the Seven Swans. "That's a national treasure, that is, and they'll have your arse if you don't paint it with the correct paint. It's got to be made to the recipe of the time for paint. Tudor-era paint."

I tossed the paintbrush from one hand to the other and eyed the wall. It looked like every matte cream-coloured wall in Britain. "How will they ever know if I use the wrong paint?"

"Oh, they'll know." Eustace nodded.

"There's an inspector, my poor old son," Stan said. "He knows everything."

"How?" I asked again.

"Well, in this case it's easy," Eustace said. "The inspector's my nephew."

"And how would your nephew know?" Even to myself I sounded a little dangerous.

"Well, I did just happen to mention it. At Sunday dinner, it was, in passing, that I told him you were doing up the old Seven Swans."

I tossed the paintbrush at the paint can. It missed, and left a smear on the broken concrete tile nearest the pub wall.

Well, there were still the flowers. "Do I have to have Tudor plants too?"

"I notice there's a red rose by the doorway," Eustace said. "It's not required, but it shows willing."

"Bah," I said.

"You seem a little out of sorts," Stan said. "Maybe you don't have the bottle for serious renovations. Good to know, before I get down to serious work. I'll not have you nitpicking every decision I make."

"I say, Stan," Eustace protested. "Go easy."

"There's a lot to know with listed renovations. You can't just put up any old thing."

I thought of the plywood bar inside the building. That shabby structure was the exact definition of the phrase *putting up any old thing*. And it was a disgusting eyesore. I pictured the fool who had got away with putting up that plywood bar in the face of listed building regulations, a fool with no love for the place. In my imagination, he had egg on his trousers, he was chewing gum, and he had his shirt untucked and hanging down behind.

I tucked my shirt in. "How do I find out about the regulations?"

"I'll get my nephew over. He'll tell you." Eustace picked up my phone. "You read up in forums. Go on and read about all the problems pub owners have had renovating Tudor-era public houses. Then after a while you give up, come to the Bearded Lamb in the village, and buy Stan and me a Guinness each and two for yourself."

"That's about right," Stan said. "Maybe two for Eustace and me and three for yourself."

I said, "I don't drink. I'm an alcoholic, if you'll remember."

"Poor lad," Stan shook his head. "Poor old fellow. Come on, Eustace, let's go and talk to that nephew of yours. Maybe he knows somebody who will work paint and plaster inside this man's budget."

"A drug addict or something?" Eustace said.

"Or a student."

"Or a student drug addict," Eustace added. "Can we stop by on our way and get a pint?" This last was whispered.

"Thanks," I said after them. I got up and set the top back onto the paint can. Then I picked up one of the petunia baskets by its hook and chain and strung it on a lower branch of a nearby willow. The weight was too much for the limb and it thumped to the ground and lay sideways. One of the petunias was broken, and the rest looked as though they'd rather be back at the shop. I sat down on the canal verge and wished that I hadn't been such a drunkard in my thirties, so that I could be one now.

CHAPTER TWO

I sat down on the tufts of grass at the river's edge, took off my shoes and socks, and slipped my feet into the water. It was bloody cold, of course, but I made myself hold them submerged. The waters moved gently, as they tend to do in Hertfordshire, with its rolling hills and complete lack of mountains. In the green-filtered light and brownish water of the river, my feet hung like dead trout. The hair on my toes and the bridge of my foot stood out darkly against white skin. When had I last gone barefoot outdoors? Nobody goes barefoot in London. It's a Browns-sandals town in summer and shiny Chelsea boots otherwise.

The last time, then, might well have been the summer that I met Holly—met her and lost her, that is. We lay together in my lightweight tent in an orchard on Crete, with our black-bottomed feet and ankles woven in and through each other's.

I heard her laugh, then. I heard her say, *Oh, Spencer, really? Like you didn't let go of Angelica? Or are you all alone on a tree-shadowed riverbank, feeling bad about your life and your own cold toes?*

I closed my eyes and remembered how brown her skin looked in that little tent, and how her breath smelled like the apples she loved to eat. The leaves on the trees by the river's edge whispered, and on the other side of the thicket a narrow boat was approaching, the engine rumbling, ropes squeaking against the gunwales. A dog coughed, and his collar jangled. It could have been forty years before, and what if I opened my eyes and my life was a dream and I was twenty and Holly was at my side? If I sat perfectly still, perhaps the past would work magic. If I didn't move, didn't think of anything like computers or mobile phones or . . .

With exasperating timing my phone rang.

I peered down at the caller's name, sighed, and answered. "Want me, Angelica, do you?"

I expected invective, but received silence.

"Angelica? You all right?"

I heard my ex-wife sigh. "I suppose so. Do you think, like Byron, that venetian blinds are a simple and elegant décor solution for a downstairs toilet window?"

"Do you care what I think?" I gazed around at the verdant waterway. Overhead birds sang, and the water gurgled.

Angelica clicked her tongue. "Yes. Well?"

I knew what she wanted me to say about venetians, and I

knew I would earn top Angelica points by saying it. But I had made a promise to Byron to leave my ex-wife alone, and so far, I had kept it.

I said, "Angelica, you're a sixty-year-old woman, right?" Too late, I realized my error. "I mean, I am too. Not a woman, but you're a woman. Sixty. A beautiful one."

"Hmm."

"How would a person get in contact with a beautiful sixty-year-old woman like yourself if you were somewhere out there in the world?"

"This is about that Holly of yours, isn't it? You've got a nerve."

"May I remind you, Angelica, that you left *me*?"

I expected a reply to the effect that I had kept Holly's photo in my wallet available for direct access, for forty years. But there was only silence.

And the faint sound of tapping.

I was about to tap *end call* when Angelica snapped. "There."

"Where?"

"I don't know exactly where. Looks like somewhere in the United States. There's a Holly Wilkerson Odell. With blonde hair."

I leapt to my feet, almost off the bank. "Is it ... ?" I stopped myself before saying *my Holly.*

Angelica said, "I don't know. I'm not about to *friend* the woman you carried about next to your bottom for forty years." More tapping sounds came from the phone.

"Can you describe her to me?"

"No. But I have made you a Facebook page." Angelica sounded better pleased with this action than I would have expected. "And I have sent her a friend message. And, there's a fellow our age on her banner. Could be her brother, of course. Now download the Facebook app and to hell with you."

As Angelica hung up on me, I heard Byron hailing me from the far side of the canal. He said, "Why aren't you painting?"

I held up my phone. "Angelica just called."

"Damn you!"

"She just wanted to know my feelings on venetians."

"Window treatments are the thin edge of the wedge." Byron added, "You promised."

"I kept it, too."

He gave a long low sigh, like the sound of a distant airplane. "I know."

I explained about the Facebook page, and he said that he would install the app, so that I could see Holly. I mentioned that there was a man in the picture. He said, "He's probably her husband. So, don't hope too hard."

Byron was right. Still, the thing about hope is that it will have its little way.

I left him fiddling with my phone and rambled off, around the outside of the Seven Swans, to a spot where the sunshine was strong enough to convince me that although it was April, June would soon be here. I sat down on the ground where grass met brick wall and leaned back. I pushed up the sleeves of my jacket to get a little more sun on my skin. It felt good. I tell myself stories, and just now could imagine that I had everything I wanted, including the possibility of finding Holly and a life free from necessity.

I pictured myself a luckier fellow than I was. Younger. Rich. Full of derring-do.

I wrestled my wallet out of my pocket and took Holly's picture out. I looked down at her. Why did I ever let you go? I wondered. How could I have allowed you to get on the bus in Heraklion? I should have stuck to you like glue, should have gone home with you to England, should have taken you back to Canada with me. I am wiser now, I thought. If I could be as old as I am on the inside, but go back in time and be twenty on the outside, I'd have the courage to hang onto my lovely Holly and never let her go.

I closed my eyes.

CHAPTER THREE

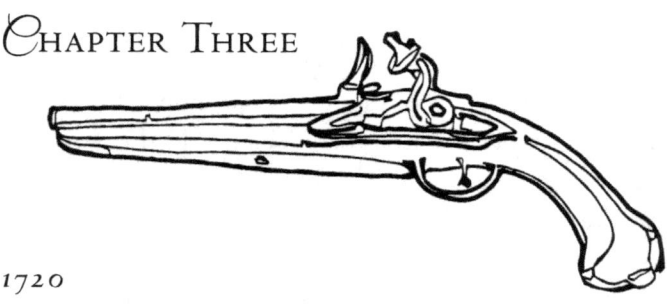

1720

I call her the Lady Highwayman, but Charlotte Ramsey is known to all in Buckinghamshire as the Swan, because she is graceful, and because people believe she's mute. When she is the Swan, rumour says her husband lets her out of her tower room in their manor house only to parade her about his lands in their elegant carriage, while his small farmers stand by the side of the road, mud caked to the knees, pressing their hats to their hearts. I've been away from my home here for two years learning the law, and so I meet her for the first time at night, and in the freedom of this moonless night, on horseback, she wears no lace or silk, and no gentlewoman's soft curls and bows around her head either. Her hair is tweaked straight back and clubbed at the neck. A cloak of coarse red wool that looks black at night enfolds her narrow torso, and she wears men's trousers stuffed into men's boots and stirrup leathers for a belt. A pistol shines at each hip.

As for me, I'm out this night riding on my horse Nettles, free for the first time in the week since my hangdog return from London, my parents having left me for a few days in London. They bade me lock our doors and stay inside with the servants, but servants are paid to watch the house and I am not. Thus, I think it fair to take my sturdy old mount and go off on my own.

That first night on the road to Aylesbury, Charlotte Ramsey only speaks to me because I'm a highwayman, too, or at least I'm considering becoming one. She trots past me and draws up her horse. She looks me up and down, from my spurs to my face to the cock of my hat. Her eyes shine like the stars overhead.

Here is what she says to me: "I can see in your love-struck gaze, sir, that you are too soft-hearted for a highwayman."

And the first thing I say to Charlotte Ramsey, is, "Your pistol butts are too well polished for caution, Lady. Even starlight will give you away."

"Are you Jack?" she asks me.

"I might be Jack," I answer cautiously. Caution was my tutor in London, where they tried to teach me law. But although I learned to speak Caution's language, I've not yet learned always to follow its course, so here I am in the black of night, unarmed, facing a woman who scolds and puts her hands on her pistols, clearly ready to pull them out and fire.

She says, "If you are Byways Jack, then you're a murderer many times over, and you will be sorry you've brought your black heart to Buckinghamshire, for the men of the county are out to hang you this very night."

I say, "Then surely I'm not Jack."

"You don't sound entirely certain." She pulls out one of her flintlocks and points it at my waistcoat.

Nettles is old but not a fool, and at the sound of the pistol cock, he takes a step backward, one shoe crunching on rock at the side of the road. I am not armed. I'm debating whether to tell her so — it would prove that I am certainly not the highwayman Byways Jack, but admitting that I with my London ways had come out without so much as a rusty matchlock would also put me at a certain disadvantage with a pistol-friendly woman — when a noise of furious riding makes itself heard and we turn towards it. Then, like dancers at a ball who know each other's movements, we race into the darkness of the trees.

We see the dozen or so mounts tear by, all the riders but one well-cloaked. We are close enough to make out the features and form of the man in the middle of the group tied by his neck to his horse. The moon gleams, and the branches drop a little in the breeze of their passing.

Now, I don't claim to know much, but I do know that men on horses galloping past with a captive tied at the neck is not a scene to be mentioned in polite society. Either they are a cutthroat gang with a victim, in which case *there but for the grace of God go I;* or they are vigilantes, protecting the peace from a lone brigand, in which case *thank God that the county Justice didn't call on me to join the vigilantes.* This would be a very good moment to make the safe choice of a polite goodnight and offer to see the Lady home.

Instead I ask, "Who was that captive, tied by the neck?"

"That was Byways Jack. So you're not he. But are you a highwayman?"

I know what I am: an uninspired student of the law. But, in a pregnant moment like this one, before my answer is given, I might be anything in the world—a foreign prince, an accountant, or a bold and uncaptured highwayman. To make this moment last, I smile and say nothing.

She growls like a lovely dog. "Have the courage to tell me truly. Are you one of us?"

This is the moment to tell her that I'm unarmed, but I let it pass. They teach you logic at law, so I ask myself, how difficult can it be to become a highwayman? It's not as if I'd have to register myself with a guild.

I decide on the spot to transform a lie into the truth, if only for this one night.

I say, "Look at me, mounted at midnight, at which hour there is no possible errand that could send an honest man about the roads. Of course I am a highwayman. How can you doubt it?"

"I can doubt anything, thank you very much, sir."

I bow.

She says, "There are only two reasons to become a highwayman. One is bloodlust. The other is desire for money. Which is it for you?"

I look at her in her holey wool and leather straps, face silvered by moonlight, eyes like stars, and do not tell her my thought, that here is a third reason to become a highwayman.

But I say, "Because I want money." And that is true enough.

She nods sharply. "And, how many forays have you under your belt?"

I say, "I tire of all these questions."

"That means a thousand forays, or none. I wager none. Come. We will pursue your first adventure. And, if you care for your neck at all, silence is the rule."

She urges her horse towards the road. I follow, anticipating that she will turn right, in the opposite direction from that the men with their captive took. Why chase after hangers of highwaymen, when one is a highwayman oneself? As well, it's only logical to fill the vacuum that Byways Jack left when he was captured. But she directs her mount left. And as she does so, I see clearly that the only sensible move is to save becoming a highwayman for a less dangerous night. I should gallop right towards home, climb into my bed, and allow the warm hand of sleep to settle upon my forehead.

Charlotte waves me towards her. I mount, but stop still at the side of the road, my hand on Nettles's cantle, gazing from left to right and then back again. My hesitation isn't due to only her beauty, for there are, at a conservative count, a thousand beautiful women in London. There's also the fact that although my family is wealthy, I do secretly need money quite fiercely, having gambled away every penny of the student's allowance my father bestowed upon me.

Gah! I head left, after Charlotte.

Charlotte casts a bright look over her shoulder at me and then kicks her mount to a gallop. I follow her out of the woods, past Seldon's properties, and then off the road through woods striped black and silver with trees and shadows. There she reins in her horse, and I rein in Nettles. I know the area well enough, and am not comforted by the thought that nearby is a sturdy tree from which, in a pinch—when there's no army nearby to do it for them—the good citizens of these parts have for hundreds of years hanged cutthroats and other rogues. We dismount, and Charlotte opens the large wallet tied flat against her saddle. She shows me how to tie a special knot, which she calls the Highwayman's Hitch. And so, I learn the first secret of the highwayman's trade, which is how to tie a quick-release knot against a perilous getaway.

I murmur, "A neat trick."

Charlotte gives me a look that reminds me of her silence rule. We leave the horses at our backs and make our way from shadow to shadow the fifty yards or so to the clearing where I have from time to time seen men, and once a woman, pendant from this tree. None are hanging there just now with blackened skin and pointed toes, but the men we saw earlier on the road are gathered beneath its branches. A few are holding the horses for the rest. The rest are holding Jack, or watching him. One man is trying the lower branches of the tree for strength, with the clear goal of climbing it.

The trees thin about us as we near the clearing. Charlotte throws herself to the ground and creeps closer. I follow. We pause behind a fallen branch, happily far enough away that the vigilantes aren't likely to see us in the shadows, and watch the preparation for hanging the highwayman, rogue, and murderer Byways Jack.

As if she reads my thoughts, Charlotte breaks her own rule of silence. She murmurs, "Do we feel sorry for Byways Jack, who kills and robs for bloodlust? Was he not once a pretty child at his mother's knee? Still, he's a black-hearted fellow."

"What proof have you of his crimes?" I ask. As a student of the law, I'm not overly fond of executions without trials.

"My husband has told me all the reports of Byways Jack

and his crimes. That's my husband over there. With the white waistcoat under his black cloak."

Moonlight illuminates not only her husband, but the dozen or so men around him by the hanging tree, several of whom have hold of Byways Jack.

"So is this my first lesson in your trade, then? Beware of being caught, young highwayman? See the fellow dangle, next time it might be me?"

"No. Now, listen, you …"

I tell her my name.

"I know who you are, Spencer. You've been studying in London since before I wed Hugh. Your parents dine with us."

"And you are Charlotte." It seems a little late for introductions, but we highwaymen must choose whether to be low or high behaved. "The Lady Charlotte, who can't speak or hear."

"Ha." Charlotte casts a self-satisfied look at me. "Unless in disguise, as you see me now, I've not said more than twenty words aloud to the world since the day my family arranged for me to marry Hugh. I thought that might end things between us, but a wife who won't speak suits him to the ground. He has tastes that keep him away nights, and, as you see, so do I."

"How did he ever win you? With money?"

"Like his loyal wastrels?" She laughs. "No, with conjuring tricks." I stare.

"It's true. He would pull flowers out of my ears and silk sleeves out of his nose. I thought with clever gentle hands like that he would be kind to me. And now you know what no one does, for I must trust the fellow at my side when we are on adventure, sir."

Lying on my stomach, in the moon's shadow, I make a horizontal bow. "Your servant, madam. And now that I know your secret, it's only fair to tell you mine: I have gambled away the allowance my father gives me." I decide to tell her the rest. "Along with the best part of my future inheritance."

Over at the hanging tree, two men are searching Jack's cloak, pulling it out from under his bonds, calling out and tossing to others various items they find in his pockets.

Chapter Four

There's a lot of chatter going on among the Baron's men now, after their earlier silence. We're too distant to hear what they're saying, but from the laughter, at least one of them is easy with his jokes. The kind of man Charlotte's husband is likely to invite to dinner, to keep the banter clever and light. Just over the Baron's head, a man is scrambling up the hanging tree, and there is some business going on with the rope dangling and tangling in the branches.

"Who are those others with your husband, those younger fellows rushing around with ropes, and two up the tree? I can't make out their faces."

"You must know them. They are of an age with you, give or take, and many were born around here, to wealthy families. They are my husband's men. I call them the wastrels."

It is what my father will call me, when he learns I've lost his money. "What makes them so loyal to the Baron, then?"

"He lends them money."

"Tied, then. But not loyal."

"He lends them money at a low interest. They redeem themselves in their families' view. And they pay him back."

"Do they?" I try to imagine how I would pay back such a loan, unless by a life of crime. "How?"

"I don't know. He enjoys their loyalty, and as far as I care, they're welcome." She glances at my side and frowns. "Where are your pistols?"

That's right—I haven't told her I'm unarmed. "You said to be quiet. Pistols aren't quiet."

"Do you have a knife?"

I shake my head. She rolls her eyes and passes me a hunting knife, unsheathed. "When you catch him, find out whether he still has my necklace, that he stole from my husband. It was my dowry jewels. Sapphires and a dangle shaped like a star."

I blink down at the knife in my hand.

She crawls a little way off to the left and gestures me to proceed to the right. "You do at least know what to do with that knife?" she hisses.

I had thought we were here to watch the miserable bound creature die. But I do know what to do with the knife.

I hiss back, "You said yourself Byways Jack is a murderer. So why rescue him?"

I expect her to say, for honour among thieves. But instead she answers, "Because he was once a pretty child at his mother's knee." She crawls away, swallowed by the shadows of the trees and bushes at the edge of the clearing.

And she screams.

All the men beneath the tree start and turn towards the sound.

Charlotte, still entirely hidden from view, screams again. Some of the men, her husband among them, begin to run across the clearing in our direction, and I hear the rattle of brush that is Charlotte, calling for help, leading the men away from Byways Jack under the tree. I curse her idea, for to run across the clearing would give me away in the moonlight, as much as if I showed myself at noon on a sunny Easter Day. The only way to reach him is to travel around the edge of the clearing. I clutch the hunting knife in my right hand and raise my left to cover my face so that its pale shape doesn't draw the interest of the two or three vigilantes who are still under the tree with Byways Jack, holding the ropes they mean to hang him with. I hope that my dark clothing and the movement of the shadows around the perimeter of the area, of branches thrown up and down by breezes, will cover my approach.

The Lady's scream sounds again, from behind me now, and I curse as the men under the trees turn their heads in my direction. One of them calls, "Can you see her?"

I realize they're addressing me. I make a negative gesture and dive back under the trees, hurrying to come out behind them.

When I do, their backs are to me, for how long I don't know, but Charlotte screams again, and some of the men call out for the Lady, as well, and that keeps these fellows standing guard looking outward. Just behind them, nearer me, I see Byways Jack, his hands tied behind him, staring outwards as well. I slink up behind the hanging tree, keeping its massive trunk between me and the Baron's men. I examine as well as I can from a few feet away the thick ropes that bind his arms and legs. I test the blade of Charlotte's knife with one thumb. It's sharp enough to skin eels, but can I count on having at least thirty seconds to slice through those bonds without the guards turning? In the silence after Charlotte's scream, one of them turns back to Byways Jack, tugs at his bonds, then turns away again. I remember the man up above, and look up to see his silhouette seated on a branch over the heads of the guards, ropes looped about his arms, watching the woods across the clearing.

Charlotte screams for help again. Bushes crash. Somebody shouts, "I see her." I slip the knife into my belt at my back, grit my teeth, and dash forward. I catch Jack by the ropes binding his arms and yank him back into the bushes, both hands behind me to haul his weight. I feel like a whipped ox on the harrow. Still, I give the blackguard credit: he doesn't make a peep while I do it, and I take some credit too, for he weighs about what I imagine my horse Nettles weighs. No cry of discovery has yet rung out — Charlotte is giving her noises a good soldier's effort. I hope it's not because she's been caught, but there's nothing I can do but follow her wishes, dragging the thief and murderer over logs, through at least one holly bank and white-blossoming, sharp-fingered hawthorn. At last I can't hear Charlotte or the men, nor can I drag him further. I cut his bonds at wrist and calf. He stands up free.

"Thank you. That was not a happy ride, but I'm a happy man for it all the same." He pats his hips, apparently looking for his weapons, but of course they were taken. He reaches into his boot and pulls out a tiny pistol, almost too small for his hands, and points it at me.

"It's a lady's gun, sir," Byways Jack says, "but it kills very well indeed."

"I've heard of these." I clear my throat and reach behind me for the Charlotte's knife. "I understand the shot, if it pierces a man's midsection, takes longer to kill him."

"A good weapon for vengeance, really."

I agree. "But I'm not sure why you want vengeance upon me, your rescuer." Knife hand behind my back, I grip the weapon firmly. It will not be a fair fight, for he is a tried-and-true highwayman, and this is my first night at it. However, there is such a thing as beginner's luck.

He smiles, and I can see the hole where one of his teeth has been knocked out, and blood on his lip. Aside from his injuries, he is quite handsome, and his looks combine with strength, poise, blood, and his pistol to create a fearsome sight.

He waves the pistol at me. "I don't want to kill you."

"What, then?" I shift my balance slightly, hefting the knife.

He holds out the pistol. "I want your knife. Much handier for the getaway road."

Behind us, I hear the unmistakeable shouts of hunting men. I'm not going to stand here arguing with Byways Jack until they overtake us and hang us both.

I toss him my knife. "Have you got a lady's necklace — sapphires, with a dangle star?"

"Never seen it. On my honour. There must be another highwayman out there, for the news of my arrival here in Buckinghamshire travelled so quickly that they caught me before I could make tuppence."

"Am I meant to believe that?"

"Just as you like." He hands me his small pistol. "Here's the plan. I'll go right, you go left. If they catch one, the other is free, and if they nab both of us, we'll be well met again in Hell." He tears away silently through the undergrowth in his chosen direction, and I in the opposite. It takes me much of the night to get home.

CHAPTER FIVE

I wake up with my sheets wrapped around me in knots, damp against my chilled back. I wake up wishing I were not what I am, a wastrel like those fellows who hang about Charlotte's good knight of a husband, tied up in debt and doubt. But I am their inferior in courage, for they have the stomach to admit their wrong to the Baron and exchange their private shame for private loans at nil percent. Worse, I am not afraid of shame, I am afraid of losing my father's regard. What's left of it.

So I lie here staring at the ceiling and ask myself, What it is that I want? I'm not a very exciting fellow, but perhaps that's why I want to be a highwayman. Excitement is like a shining jewel somebody else owns. That's how I earned so much debt, sitting up late in the smoky dens of gamblers quicker and cleverer than I. I can't blame it on luck, even lying here in my tangled bedclothes, using my toe to push open the casement window and let in the April morning air. I believe, as some believe in salvation, that we've all got the same luck, so those other noble and near-noble gambling men must have been quicker and cleverer than I.

A wand of ivy, part of the big vines climbing the wall up and around my window, taps on a diamond-cut casement pane and reminds me of my own question. *What do I want?* The answer is *To be a highwayman and make a lot of money so that I am my own man.* And what that means is *to be hanged pretty soon*, for despite Charlotte and my successful rescue of Byways Jack, after one night I have not a cent more to my name, and I have lost my horse Nettles as well. For I remember that I perforce left him hobbled to a stone on the far side of the clearing where stands the hanging tree. I want my horse. For I can lie about where I was last night, and I can omit all mention of having gambled away my father's allowance. But I can't hide the fact that Nettles is missing.

I fight free of my bedding and throw it in the direction of the window. I walk across the floor barefoot and in my shirttails to look outside, gazing out from my room at the green sward below, which separates our home from the woods, and beyond which lie the estates of our neighbours, including many a young wastrel like myself, and the Baron's estates, where languishes silent Charlotte, when she isn't being a garrulous highwayman. I imagine polishing my boots and walking away through the woods to ask the Baron for a loan, at nil per cent, with which to pay my next season's boarding fees, and which I will repay once I become a lawyer and silver flows into my palm like rain onto a famished farmland. I wonder whether it's not a sign that I'm a lucky man that I can slip along the quiet lanes of life and take safe choices, and that these are always offered me. The Baron's generosity is just another sign of my good luck. I'm rummaging in my trunk for my shoe brushes, to spiff myself before approaching him for money, when I hear Nettles's whinny from outside below. When I run to see, he's on our green, unhitched, grazing on my mother's mint garden.

I dress myself, noting that my shirt smells somewhat, but not unendurably, of nervous perspiration after my rescue of Byways Jack. His denial of our local robberies sticks in my craw. Not because I think he was lying. I do not. I'm worried for Charlotte, because whoever perpetrated the robberies may still be out there. Last night before I slept I imagined myself finding him and taking back at pistol-point Charlotte's dowry necklace with the star dangle.

But now, in the light of day, and all dreams aside, I want my neck to stay the length it is, not stretched by any baron's rope. So I hang about the woods for much of the day, only returning to eat at lunch and dinner. I mean to tell Charlotte, when she comes for me, that I will not go with her to be a highwayman.

But she does not come. And by nightfall, I am so bored with being myself, and so dazzled by my memory of Charlotte, her hair and eyes silver in the moonlight, that I tuck Byways Jack's pistol into my boot, mount Nettles, and ride out to tell her that I will.

I find her easily on the road near the hanging tree. Her hair still shines silver, and her cloak is still ragged enough to disguise her wealthy identity. I hope. She smiles when she sees me.

"You don't mind if they hang you?" she asks.

I answer, bold as a sabre sword, "Not tonight, for I haven't robbed anybody yet."

"You freed Byways Jack. If he's caught, he will turn you in."

"Do you think so? I don't. He seemed a gentleman to me. Or once was, at least."

"So did you come to talk about robbery, or do some?" She gestures with one gloved hand at the road, dark before moonrise.

I look at her. I think of the money. I say, bold as gold guineas, "Was I afraid last night?"

"I'll tell you what." Charlotte's horse moves restlessly, as if eager to be off and holding up coaches. "Take this."

She tosses me something black, a little larger than my two hands together. I hold it up. It is a mask. She puts her own mask on, and it covers her eyes, but I can still see brightness there, and her smile.

She says, "This is good. Us together. Because ... Well, student of mine? Why?"

I say, "Because the law, or the vigilantes, will be looking for a married couple of thieves, and they will search the inns and barns for such a pair."

"Right. And you can search them and take purses and jewels, while I hold them at pistol-point. You being careful not to ... ?"

Not to ... what? I picture the scene, Charlotte standing, one trousered leg outstretched, a shining pistol in each hand pointed at a half-dozen or so quaking coach riders. Me gently removing items of value from their persons. I scowl. And then it comes to me. "I must be careful not to come between your pistol and ..."

"And our victims." She peers at me. "You don't like the word *victims*."

"It makes them sound dead," I say.

"That's entirely up to them." But she laughs.

"I'm not about to kill anybody," I tell her. "That's my worry, that they'll see right through me."

"I told you, you're too soft-hearted for a highwayman. That's why you have me, and I have the pistols."

I do have a pistol. Byways Jack's pistol, snug in my boot. Loaded. The thought of it emboldens me still more, and I ask how many forays she has made, on her own, before me.

She hesitates, and I laugh. "None at all? And you, such an expert thief?"

"I practised and scouted and learned the hours the coaches are likely to travel, and their routes," she protests. "I needed a partner. Now I have one."

"You do indeed, Lady. I apologize for laughing."

"I've done all the hard work, and you will reap the benefits."

"I certainly hope so. It seems to me that beginner's luck is more and more in play in this highwayman's life."

We gallop together along the road towards the county border, well-shadowed by trees. I wonder where we are going, but I know as if I've always known that Charlotte will not pause in her riding to answer me. She keeps her seat like a huntress queen, and I don't need to see her face to know the scowling joy upon it. Beneath me, Nettles clatters on, moving with the strength of a younger horse than he is, as if he likes the life of a highwayman's horse. And well he may, because what is gold to him compared with the scented darkness and open road?

Charlotte turns her mount off the road past the Montagues' place. The mansion windows are dark, as if all are asleep, but I've known their son Edward since childhood, and he is as much a wastrel by nature as I am, perhaps more. I want to ask Charlotte whether Edward is one of her husband's men, but I keep my tongue and ride my horse after her. We ride across the bridge that leads to the London road and as we reach the county crossing,

Charlotte leaps from her horse and I do the same. We lead our mounts into the undergrowth and stand hidden from the road as she hobbles our horses again. The whole business is rather thrilling, and nothing has even happened yet.

"What now?" I ask.

"Be silent and listen," Charlotte says. "Do you hear horses?"

I listen. But there are only branches clicking together in the light April breeze, and our own mounts, and Charlotte's breathing close at my side. "Are we listening for the vigilantes?"

I feel a small movement at my side that is Charlotte nodding. "They know as well as we that Byways Jack isn't likely to return. The vigilantes believe their job is done. So our chance tonight to get some money from travellers is good, if a late coach comes through."

"Yes. But your husband is rich. Why do you want money?"

"Why indeed. Have you met Hugh?"

"Do you mean you wish to escape marriage to him?"

She laughs. "Perhaps. I rather enjoy this night-time game, though."

We stand and wait. The night is not warm, and I gather my coat around me and stand close to Nettles for warmth, and Charlotte does the same with her own horse. We stand some more. We listen: to the breeze, to a blackbird in the distance up late and singing hard. And at last we hear the hoof beats and the jingle and crack of a coachman's whip that mean a coach is coming. I jerk forward in anticipation, and Charlotte puts a steadying hand on my shoulder.

"Let me do the talking," Charlotte says.

"That is good sense. Since you never speak, your voice will not be recognized."

"And I enjoy the talking," Charlotte says. "I have a bold way about me when I wear a mask."

"Only when you wear a mask?" I joke. The coach is near, now. Unseen under cover of trees and undergrowth, unseen the moon has cleared the horizon and lights the scene before us.

"Ready on my count of three. One. Two."

I begin my leap to land in front of the approaching coach. She thrusts out her arm and stops me.

"It's my husband's carriage," she hisses. "Someone of his guests may recognize me."

"Damn," I hiss. And, "Sorry."

"Blaspheme away," she says over the noise of wheels. "We're highwaymen, not ministers."

But the coachman pulls his horses up just about where we would have halted. The Baron's coachman leaps down from his seat with a creak of leather against wood and the rattle of stones under the soles of his boots. In two steps, his coat swirling around him, he has the coach door open and hauls one of his passengers out. The fellow falls on hands and knees in the gravelled road and vomits loudly.

"Better out than in, young fellow," the coachman says in surprisingly cultured tones. "And better out of the coach than in it. I ought to leave you here."

I look questioningly at her, but she shakes her head. I keep still.

The drunken fellow mumbles thanks as the coachman hauls him, drooping, to his feet. I can make out a couple of passengers inside the coach, peering out. The young fellow wipes his mouth with his sleeve and makes for the open coach door. I have felt like he does now and then, and I'm sure he'd give a limb just at this moment to lie down on the bench seat within and fall asleep.

But the coachman, who no doubt has enough to do without cleaning sick off his employer's leather seats, pulls him round to the back of the carriage and hoists him onto the footman's perch. He bids the drunken fellow to hold on tight. But no sooner has the coach moved out of sight than we hear the thud of a falling body and a shout of agony, followed by the diminishing noise of horses and coach riding away in the distance.

We leap up and, leaving our horses, run together along the road towards the cry.

"Masks on or off?" I gasp.

"On," she answers. "And I will stay out of sight. If the coach returns I must hide myself quickly."

"Will the passengers recognize you?" I ask. "When you're wearing your mask?"

"The passengers might not, but the coachman may. That was my husband, enjoying himself with whip and bridles, driving his own coach."

CHAPTER SIX

I know the fellow lying on the roadway by sight. He's the son of a man with a lovely big house in town. His name is Hal, and he is sprawled so wide across the gravelly roadway that for a moment I fear he's dead. But he moves his hand, and then his arm, reaching up inside the breast as if to check for money, or a gun. I touch my mask to be sure it covers my eyes, tug up the collar of my coat, and pull down the brim of my hat.

"Hal?"

"I have the money safe with me, father," he mumbles, his eyes shut tight. His breath is red with wine. "And at very low interest."

At the sound of his voice, I hear Charlotte draw the horses closer.

"Wait here, and I'll take care of you," I tell Hal. I run for Nettles and make Hal get up on my horse, which must be a comical struggle for Charlotte to witness. I leave Hal draped across Nettles's saddle and approach her in the shadows. "Will we try again tomorrow night?"

"Yes."

"Do you vow it? Come hell or high water?" I ask.

"Or both together. I wouldn't miss our next try for anything."

I ride, with Hal snoring in front of me, to his father's house. I set him down outside the door. He thanks me, calling me Sir Highwayman. I am climbing back into Nettles's saddle when he begins to pat at his coat breast again. He lets out a cry of fury.

"Thief! Where's my money?" He takes hold of my heel.

"I didn't take anything from you." I jerk free, and he snatches at Nettles's bridle.

"You stole the Baron's loan to me. You've taken it, every penny."

"You're still drunk." No doubt the money he'd borrowed from the Baron at a low interest is somewhere about him. Still, to be sure, I ride back the way we came and search the place he fell, but find nothing there. Perhaps Charlotte picked it up. I will ask her tomorrow night.

But when night follows day, and I ride out to meet her, she isn't at the hanging tree. I wait two full hours, until moonrise, and then ride through the woods to the Baron's house to find out why.

CHAPTER SEVEN

Not everything gossiped in town about the Baron's Lady is true. For example, I know now that Charlotte can speak and hear. But she does live in a tower in the older section of Baron Hugh Ramsey's great house. I stand looking up at it, holding Nettles's reins, and after a moment there is a rustle in the trees by the near side of the great house. I turn to greet her.

But I hold my tongue just in time, for it is not Charlotte. Her husband the Baron joins me.

"A good night, Spencer," he says.

"You know me?" I ask, glad it's dark so he won't perceive my nervousness.

"I know your father."

"Yes. Pleased to meet you." I was ready to be a highwayman tonight, and now must act like a student. I can see that some sort of explanation is necessary for my presence on his grounds. At night.

I say, "I am interested in stars and their formations."

"Do I have the best stars, then?" He gestures at the sky above his property.

I shrug. "I followed a falling star and it led me here."

"I hope you wished on it."

"I'm more of a scientist. And a man of law."

He laughs, and it sounds genuine.

"You have lovely grounds," I add. "I suppose you come out often?"

"Occasionally. A man should look at what is his."

The light in Charlotte's tower goes out.

He says, "We are lucky to be men, with large concerns."

"Like finance," I suggest.

"And justice," he agrees.

I see a dark figure moving in the ivy, moving down. To draw his attention from the tower, I point up at the sky. "Do you know the name of that star?"

"No." He's not looking at the star. He's peering at Charlotte's tower. "Spencer, what are you doing here? Why have you come?"

Why would I come to his property? "I am here to ask you for a loan."

He gazes thoughtfully at the tower. "Come tomorrow night. I take it you would like to leave your father out of things?"

"That would be ideal."

The black shape is out of sight. He says, "The ivy on that tower must be dealt with."

I clear my throat. "I think it looks lovely."

"I do not. I think I will go and say goodnight to my wife."

I want to say, Let her sleep. But that would sound proprietary. As if she were mine and not his.

As if I had spoken, he answers thoughtfully, "I found something of hers. I believe she will sleep better if she has it back." And although there is no reason to show this thing to me, he holds out a handful of diamonds, the star-shaped dangle hanging over the side of his palm.

"Pretty," I say. I stop myself from saying another word.

"Come to us at eight o'clock. We'll number about a dozen for supper." He puts the necklace in his pocket.

As he leaves, he raises a hand in farewell. I hear a crackle in the bushes.

She says, "Hail, colleague of the night."

I say, "Charlotte. I think your husband saw you climbing down the ivy."

"No. How could he be sure?" She moves closely and grips my arm. "The trees are moving in the wind. I might have been a shadow."

"Perhaps. But he'll soon know. He's on his way to you now."

She wastes not a second running through the shadows, and I soon see her form swinging up the vines and through the window. The lamp comes on, and Nettles and I make our way home.

CHAPTER EIGHT

The ivy is chopped down from Charlotte's tower when I return the next night to get dinner and a loan at low interest from the Baron. Charlotte will not be leaving by the window, tonight or any night.

I stand in the Baron's foyer while the Baron's servant takes my coat and hat. I watch where he hangs it, in a vestibule just inside the front door, among a lot of other coats much like mine, with the bit of an extra cape about the shoulders that all we young men are wearing this year.

"Please join the others," the servant says, and maybe I'm imagining the scorn in his tone.

"Indeed, that's what I'm here to do," I reply.

My boots are not what the world expects from evening dress, but when I enter the Baron's library and see the young wastrel guests standing about, busily drinking from the Baron's decanters, I'm not alone in wearing boots. I doubt whether the others have a highwayman's mask and a small pistol tucked into their boot-tops, though.

I'm swarmed by these young men. Some are friends of my youth Edward Montague, and a cousin of the Seldons I remember from long ago. Several are new to the area, and one is the young fellow from mine and Charlotte's adventure two nights ago. Hal is sober tonight. He looks miserable, although he has friends all around him. The library is ablaze with light from many-armed candelabras. Through a pair of double doors there stands the great dining table, set for the company. Beyond is a line of the new French doors. It is certainly a grand display, and a great improvement upon

the house as it looked when the old Baron had it: grey, cold, and on the shabby side.

Sitting at table alone, apparently awaiting the guests, I see Charlotte. She's dressed as the Baron's Lady, in lace and her hair in curls, her starry necklace around her neck. I don't think she sees me.

I count a baker's dozen of us young men here in the library. The Baron must be rich indeed to afford all this and give loans at low interest to all of us here. He must have inherited the money, but from whom? Not the old Baron, unless all this money was in a treasure chest, unspent. I suppose it's possible.

"Here's to Spencer," Edward Montague says aloud, and the others raise their glasses.

"Do you know Hal?" Edward asks me. "Poor fellow! Robbed two nights back, and all the Baron's loan moneys in his pocket."

"Don't worry, dear Hal," the Seldon cousin says from behind his cup of red wine. "It's a tragedy, of course, but Ramsey will give you more time to pay. And another loan, if you want it. Same low interest."

Hal looks up hopefully. "It happened to you, too, didn't it?"

"Yes. And to Montague here."

I look from one to the other. "Should I fear robbery too, if the Baron lends me the money I need?"

"No more than the rest of us," says the fellow with the wine.

"No less than the rest of us," says Montague. "But, never worry, Spencer, there are other solutions."

"The rash of household robberies," Hal says gloomily. The others laugh at what is clearly an inside joke.

A voice says, "Welcome all. Come in to supper."

The Baron stands in the doorway smiling, his eyes searching the crowd. His gaze alights on me, and he steps towards me, taking my hand and making me a special welcome.

He leads me into the dining room shining with dark wood and white dishes, and presents me to Charlotte.

Charlotte nods to me, to all of us, but of course she doesn't speak. Her husband doesn't stop. As soup is served to us all out of a tureen shaped like a wild boar with leaves for ears, the Baron holds us rapt with stories of the rising of 1715. Then, over the meat and more wine, he tells of his good luck when so many about him lost their moneys to the South Sea Bubble. The French windows that will in warm months stand open to the grounds begin to steam a little, and I think about the size of this property and how much it must cost to maintain it.

I ask, "How did you manage to hold your fortune, my lord?"

He replies jovially, "I didn't gamble it away, young man."

The whole bunch of us laugh in what ought to be, but is not, a sheepish manner. Charlotte smiles into the glass of wine before her and toys with her food.

The Baron takes a last bite of beef before the plates are cleared. He says to the table at large, "What do you say, the lot of you? Do you agree that Spencer here is a good risk and a hearty fellow who will repay what is owed?"

Hal looks gloomy, but raises his glass with the rest, saying, "Aye."

By the time we've finished our supper the wine is sitting heavily, but so is the beef, so I'm keeping upon my feet. Charlotte hasn't eaten, but I think I'm the only one who's noticed it. It doesn't matter. After two hours with the Baron and his young wastrel friends, my mind is spinning with potentials.

The Baron rises at the end of the table. He smiles at everyone, ending with me, and beckons to a servant, who stands ready with a tray upon which stands a very large wine glass — it looks as if it could hold several cups — and a leather wallet, with his initials on it.

He says, "Drink the wine and take the money."

I thank him, and the servant sets the wallet and the wine in front of me. This is truly an enormous wine glass. No wonder Hal was drunk the night Charlotte and I found him, the night he said we robbed him. I gaze from the wine to the wallet to Charlotte, smiling and silent on the far side of the table. I want to ask her just how her spendthrift husband got so much money to lend these young men at low interest.

And why should he lend us this money, anyhow? For his is not the mien of a philanthropist. Furthermore, while I see that he likes being the centre of this youthful gathering, he's not one of those fellows who needs adulation but simply enjoys it as he enjoys good beef. Therefore, there's something more going on in this room.

Is the Baron putting together an army for political reasons, or forming some sort of overseas adventure, a new company in foreign lands? No, for of all the people in the world to choose for a bold endeavour, these young fellows are the last an intelligent leader would choose. They are, like myself, good for nothing but borrowing funds at a low interest and then asking for more. But how do we pay back our loans?

A rash of household burglaries. The young fellow's laughter at their mention.

What if they would steal items from their own homes and sell them, probably in London, to pay back the Baron? And then, being short of funds again, they would do it again. Which serves them, but it still doesn't benefit the Baron. He is receiving only a very small interest from each. Not enough for him to bother with us. Not enough for splendour.

Unless . . .

I stare down at the wallet. I remember that the Baron is good at conjuring tricks. And that Hal, like the rest of these fellows, had drunk from this enormous cup. He was reeling and vomiting when we saw him climb out of the Baron's coach. Hal had Baron's loan wallet on him while he was being helped by the Baron onto the back of his coach. And then, when Charlotte and I found him, he'd not had the wallet anymore. And it must have been so for others who had drunk from the cup.

I stare at the Baron. What a clever man he is, for it's rather good business to lend money at small interest and then steal the loan back. When the young fellow robs his family to repay the loan, the interest is a little more than a hundred percent, and this circle of fellows from good homes with bad spending habits will only grow. The Baron and his lady will only grow richer.

I sip at the large glass of wine, toast them both, and ask to be excused to make room for more wine, which remark is taken with good cheer by all. I flee the dining room and find the vestibule, luckily free from servants. I put on my coat, pull my mask out of my boot-top, and put it on, following up with my hat. And I take out my pistol, and hold it ready.

CHAPTER NINE

I run out of the Baron's vestibule, out the front door and round to the left to the grounds in front of the dining room. My coat flies out around me, and I fire my pistol at the sky. I hear, from inside, the cry of "Thief!" Others shout, "It's he! The brigand, the robber, the highwayman!" The dining room French doors bang open, and as the Baron and his men pour out in pursuit, I'm already back inside the front door. I run through the library and into the dining room, where Charlotte sits alone. She is laughing, and I want to laugh too, but the men will soon return.

"I'm going to leave Buckinghamshire," I say to Charlotte. "Do you want to come with me?"

She nods. Still she doesn't speak.

We both look at the open windows. And to the wallet.

"Shall I take it?" I ask. For this is still her dining room, until she leaves it with me.

For the first time tonight, she speaks. "Of course, take it. Are we not highwaymen?"

And she hurries me out the back way, to our horses.

CHAPTER TEN

We gallop hard for the first hour, through the secret ways Charlotte knows from her nights outside. We ride along the London road, listening for hoof beats behind us. I wonder how soon we'll have to make a dash into the countryside to evade the Baron and his men. But he doesn't come, and now our horses ride side by side, and she offers me her hand. I take it. "Perhaps the Baron doesn't want to lose face by telling people that his wife has left him."

"He is proud like that," she says.

"Or it could be that he knows that we know that he's milking those young wastrels, and doesn't want to spoil his future gains. Perhaps he's stopped any chase already, and will let us go to London, and write us off as a loss."

Charlotte says, "I don't want to go to London."

"We'll have your husband's money to live on."

"I don't want his money."

There's a pause. I don't say, Then why did you tell me to take it? Instead, I say, "Charlotte, money is like the river up ahead. It flows through and around people, without taking on the shape of them. Money stays pure, though people don't."

She shoots a narrow look my way. "Well, I don't want it. And anyway, we have my necklace to sell."

I sigh. "Lucky you got it back."

"He probably pawned my dowry necklace to get his first loan," she says. "He was becoming so rich that he redeemed it and gave it back to me."

I agree. She falls silent. I numerate to myself the reasons why we should keep the wallet with the Baron's money in it. But she is so lovely, and I am so lucky to ride beside her with my hand in hers, that I agree. "If you don't want to go to London, then where? Shall we keep to the countryside and be highwaymen?"

"No, for as you've pointed out, my husband, when he was stealing back his loans, was a sort of highwayman, and then we'd be like him."

"Yes." I remembered how her husband had tried to hang Byways Jack and pin the robbery on him.

She points ahead. "I have decided that when we cross that bridge, he will no longer be my husband."

I nod. "But you'll have explain that to the priest that marries us."

"No, for I have also decided that you and I will be married when we've crossed that bridge."

"Right." I sigh. "What do we do with the money, then?"

"Throw it off the bridge," says Charlotte. "That way, we will be free of the Baron entirely by the time we cross to the other side of it."

I bow. We walk on until we reach the middle of the bridge. Once there, I see we are not alone.

A sad-looking fellow of about forty, wearing a city clerk's garb and a hat too big for him, leans over the wall of the bridge, looking down into the black water.

"Here's what we do with the money," Charlotte says.

I gaze at her with awe. "A perfect thought, wife."

"I'm not your wife until we cross the far side of this bridge." She halts her horse and climbs down. I follow.

She says, "Why so sad, sir?"

He looks up at her. He takes off his hat. "Lady, I want to go back to London."

She smiles. "What's stopping you?"

He can't help smiling back at her. "A generous inheritance sends me to Hertfordshire."

Charlotte's face falls. I squeeze her hand, for I know that she wanted to surprise him with the Baron's money, and the news that this sad fellow has money already is a heavy disappointment.

But the man in clerk's clothing is shaking his head no. "If only it were money, I'd be dancing over this bridge instead of wishing it were high enough to jump from. No, I've inherited a building and a business in the country." He reaches into the bosom of his coat and takes out a folded bit of parchment and makes as if to throw it into the river.

"Sir, can't you sell it?"

"Not tonight, I can't. And by tomorrow, I'll be caught up in the business way of thinking, and go to Hertfordshire instead of London, and live a life in the country, and marry a widow with pushy children, and live my life second best."

I take the Baron's money from his leather wallet. I toss the wallet off the bridge into the water. "You can live in London with this," I say. "Go on, take it."

"If you'll take the business?" When we nod, the look in his eyes is like an angel's blessing upon our less than licit betrothal.

He has pen and ink, and, business done, we stroll together to the end of the bridge, leading our horses. As luck would have it, the late coach from Whistler's Inn passes soon thereafter, and we see him safely onboard it. Then we kiss, for we are married now, says Charlotte.

"And, what are we?" I ask.

"Married," she repeats.

"I know that, but what are we in Hertfordshire? What did we buy?"

She holds the document out to catch a pool of moonlight to read by. "We are publicans."

"Are we?" I blink. I try to imagine the previously silent Charlotte at a bar, pouring drinks for travellers and chatting happily and at length with the trade. "Will you like that?"

"I will, if you will."

"We'll have to give up our guns," I say.

"We can keep a pistol behind the bar," she allows. "In case of robbers."

"Done," I tell her. "But let's not shoot Byways Jack, no matter what."

"Done."

"And, one more thing." I'm not at all sure how she will feel about this. "I would like to return the Baron's loan, including the low interest."

"He doesn't need it. Or deserve it."

"I'm a student of the law, Charlotte. Or, I was. We can send it secretly, by messenger, at night."

Charlotte's face lights. "Oh, Spencer, let's take the Baron his money ourselves, from time to time, masked and at midnight."

"We'll ride across the county lines under the moon, in honour of the black and memorable nights we rode out together into peril and crime."

"Done and done and done."

We mount up with a swirl of skirts—hers—and coat—mine. And we gallop off along the moonlit road to Hertfordshire.

CHAPTER ELEVEN

The sun had gone behind a cloud. I shivered and realized that Byron was shaking me awake.

"Stop that, confound you." I gazed up at him. I was not fully myself still, and asked him, "Why don't I meet you in these mysteries in time, Byron?"

He peered at me. "Are you going around the bend, old pal?"

"Well, I guess you're a wastrel ..." I held up my hand as he began to protest. "And so am I. Did Eustace get in touch with his listed-building-inspector nephew?"

"I've no information on that score, but you have a friend request on your new Facebook page. From Angelica. That was quick." He scowled at me. "Shall I accept?"

I sighed. It had never been difficult to encourage Angelica when she was with Byron. "No."

"Good." He swore. "I've accepted by accident! Now, there are two more friend requests, and brace yourself, they are from a woman and a man who look from their pictures to be about our age."

"Where?"

"In the States."

"Heavens above." I sat up. "Is it Holly?"

"Possibly. And it looks like the other is her husband. Morgan Odell, married to Holly Wilkerson."

Above our heads a heron cried and dived out of a tree at some kind of prey—a fish, going about its own business with no idea of being snapped up for a snack, or a frog, happily singing its guttural song.

I sighed. "Okay. How do I accept Holly's husband's friendship?"

"The *accept* button, here."

I hesitated. I reached out my hand for the phone.

Byron pulled it away from me. "Look, Spencer. As an actual, in-the-flesh friend I must intervene. We hoped Holly would not be married. And Holly is married. I'm worried that you will be sad, and if you are sad, you will drink."

"I'm not sad. Why would I be sad?" I asked bitterly. "I have a new friend with a wonderful wife."

Byron's eyebrows rose. "I say. Would you come between man and wife?"

Now, Byron himself had come between man and wife.

"I'm just going to make sure Holly's happy. Does she look happy?"

Together we leaned over the phone and gazed down at the picture of Holly at sixty.

"She's pretty," Byron pronounced.

"That wasn't my question."

"She's smiling." But he sounded doubtful. "Still, if you're be-friending her husband, old sport, remember what's cricket."

"Cricket, forsooth." I shot him a look. "Let us not forget that I'm still married to the woman you're living with."

He coughed. "Regarding that touchy spot between us, I think we agreed that points are about even over the course of a long friendship." He ambled off towards the canal, phone out, no doubt calling Angelica to give up the venetian blinds.

I sucked my lip and stared down at Holly's lovely face. At sixty, I'd still know her anywhere. I'd still know her smile. And for once, I was glad that our relationship, at twenty, had not been without friction and misunderstandings. Because I knew her face when it was truly happy, and I knew how she looked when she was only pretending to be. And Holly, in this picture, seated by her husband, was pretending.

The question was, for how much longer was she planning to pretend? Forever, or just for now?

I looked down at the smiling fellow at her side. Exactly what had this Morgan fellow done to make Holly pretend? I thought of the Baron, who was real and not real. And remembered Charlotte, who looked so much like Holly. I looked up at the brickwork of the Seven Swans and asked aloud, "These lives I lead from your past must mean something, mustn't they?"

A blackbird sang out, tunefully and at length. The Seven Swans, naturally, stood silent.

I pressed *accept*. Holly and Morgan Odell had a new friend.

§

Spencer Stevens will return in 'The Bridgewater Canal Mystery' *in* Pulp Literature *Issue 16, Autumn 2017.*

A WASSAIL IN INH

Nicholas Christian

Nicholas Christian's *poetry has appeared or is forthcoming in* The Lindenwood Review, Off the Coast, Poetry Quarterly, Gravel, Dămfino, *and* Panoply. *He lives in St Louis with his stuffed sea lion Gerald and his coyote Loki that thinks it's a cat. He studies at the University of Missouri-St Louis.*

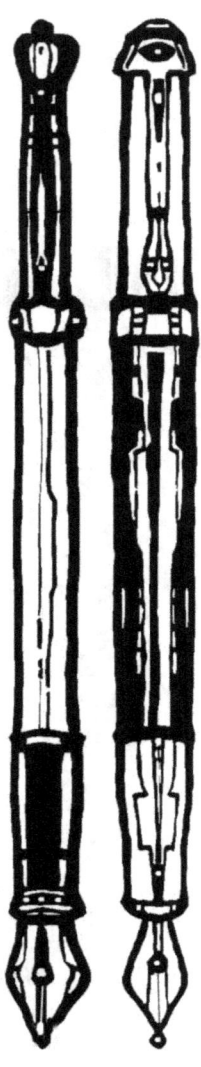

$\mathcal{A}$ Wassail in Ink

And this is its beginning:
a Vietnamese Ocean;
the bottom rim stiff with starch
grinding like rough glass
against an old belt buckle,
yes sweeping and moving
in rhythm through the dark
of a stone spiral street.

And there the cavalier waited,
iron-red mouth brushing
your waist and Avery Colt
laughed into beer
before the night church of Kansas
knew even spoiled honey
is sweet in black stilettos
under sconces of electric tallow.

Our canoe was carved for sinking,
certain your wet shoes remember
walking into the dusk of gun-fire
tasting the vanilla whorl of water lilies.
And some braveries are old tears
stranded and hungry
on island sand, and words taken
by the wind return possessions

in the rain, grown thick
and resonant as stretching pelicans—
we've landed on Bluebeard's birch table,
sure in opening one more door
the joys of hearing Rumi ask
what have I ever lost by dying?
What choice but to sentence shining
with fat our piles of bones

to the burning wood; now there is space
for the tapestry of your back
to fit my hand—learning language
through the body
set so close to the future
there is only the dance of it.
Which is all to say: these places are maps
black from all this spilled ink

collecting in my cup full of little crows
I've brought to your lips,
meaning nothing more than
we are seven words written
when not looking.

PACK UP YOUR TROUBLES

A M Soto

A M Soto is a New Zealand-based multi-genre writer. She is also a mom, cook, knitter, and sports fan. Her poem 'Northland' was published in Pulp Literature Issue 10, Spring 2016 and more of her work can be found at adamariasoto.com.

$\mathcal{P}$ACK UP YOUR TROUBLES

"What are you humming, sir?"

Dav turned to the lieutenant. He was too young for the rank, his vestigial gills not even fully closed, but no one was who they should be anymore.

"It's a song from Earth." He hadn't even realized he was humming. One of many habits he had picked up on Earth. At first it was mimicry to put the humans more at ease. Then it became something he didn't even think about.

"You must have been on Earth a long time to learn human music."

"Eight years, almost 25 of theirs." He shifted around. They were huddled in the remains of a small municipal communications office. Two walls were blasted open to the elements, while rubble covered the floor. The rain hissed as it pelted against their portable energy shield. He was sure the rain never used to fall that hard, but there never used to be the particulates of 500 ships burning up in the atmosphere. He shifted again and felt the last apple in his pocket press against his leg.

He took another bite of apple. The hyperspace com showed him Isaa drinking scotch, looking so much older than when they had first met, his hair having gone white in the human fashion.

"Go easy on that apple. I won't be able to send you more for a while."

Dav took another bite. The apple was starting to go to his head. His face was going numb, and he swore he could see moon vines growing up the walls. "I tried to stop them." He heard the hiss in his voice badly accenting his English. "I tried to talk them out of it. They didn't understand. I couldn't make them understand. They said you were too primitive to put up a defence, that they would take Earth before the third moon eclipses the fourth."

"Home by Christmas. Do you know when?"

He shook his head. Another human gesture that had become habit. "I'm out of the loop, as you would say. The council said I was too fond of you, of Earth."

Isaa poured and drank another glass. "Well, if your people do take Earth, I guess you'll get to come visit."

"Earth won't let itself get taken, at least not for long. I tried to tell the council that." He took a large bite of apple, sucking down the juice first and enjoying the cool numbness that bloomed through his body at the sweet taste.

"Either way, save those apples."

"**I hear humans** will eat their young, and each other, and you can chop off their limbs and they won't die," a sergeant sitting next to the lieutenant added.

Those were some of the more mundane rumours he'd heard about humans since the war started. The moons only knew what the humans were saying about his people. "They don't eat their young. They will eat each other if all other options are taken away." The dozen other huddled young soldiers flushed yellow. "And if they get to a doctor quickly enough, they can lose all four limbs and survive. The doctors will even give them new ones."

"That is impossible and ... unnatural."

The hospital was clean and bright for the tour. He stopped by a large window that looked down into a room containing a few particularly small human young. All of the children had at least one limb with a metallic sheen. Doctor Isaa Francis stopped with him.

"Now this we are very proud of. Every one of these children were born missing at least one limb or lost one within the first six months of their lives. With adults we've found that grafting on a cloned limb works better. However, for children who never had them, we get excellent results from these fully artificial ones."

Two of the children attempted to toss a ball between each other. They missed almost every pass. "It does take slightly longer to learn to work the limbs in tandem, because they are connected to different parts of the brain, but by the time the children start school you'd never know the difference. We cover them with a skin match polymer, and they can function as well as any other child. Better in some cases."

A child of darker complexion, like Doctor Isaa Francis, was attempting to walk the length of a thin beam on two artificial legs while holding the hand of an adult.

"Of course at this age they grow so fast they need constant recalibration and upgrades every six months." The child walking the beam reached the end and jumped into the arms of the adult. "I'm sure what you have is much more sophisticated, but we're still pretty proud of this."

Dav nodded because it seemed an appropriate gesture. His people had nothing like this. The thought of losing a limb and surviving was incomprehensible. To lose anything more than a finger, maybe a hand at most, would result in shock that would instantly shut down the brain while the body frantically tried to pump blood to the missing limb. They had never researched limb replacement, because no one had ever survived losing one.

"You should be proud of this, Doctor Isaa Francis."

"You know, Ambassador, you've known me a month. I think you can call me Isaa."

Dav found himself humming again.

"What is that song?" someone asked from the far side of the group. A civilian, if it could be said there were civilians anymore. Even he had been drafted in, in these last days.

"It's a song about war."

"Humans sing songs about war?"

"Yes. I think half their songs are about war. They sing about war being good and war being bad. They have songs about people going to war, and about the people they leave behind, and songs about coming back from war, or not."

"You cannot go *to war with Earth," Dav pleaded to the Grand Council. It never used to be like this. The high arches of the debate chamber, meant to show the light of the five moons, now felt like the fingers of a giant hand squeezing down.*

"We have read your reports, Ambassador. They have only had slip technology for their ships for ten years."

"That's 30 of theirs. They can do a lot in 30 years. They already have dozens of colonies."

"Poorly defended. Physically they are weak. They are prone to injury and illness. They have no personal armour. Their weapons are based on either lasers or small bits of metal projected through the air."

"Our battle leaders are projecting we can take over Earth in less than a year," said one of the few remaining councillors not in a uniform.

Dav wanted to crack his own head against the council members. Drive some sense into them. They simply didn't understand.

"They sing songs about war," Dav shouted.

"What does that have to do with anything?"

"Everything! They wage war on each other at every possible opportunity then sing songs about it."

"They are weak barbarians."

"They are highly adaptable survivors and rapid breeders." He pressed the flats of his hands together, a human gesture never seen on his world. "They sing songs about war."

Dav shifted and felt the apple in his pocket. There was another flash in the sky. It may have been lightning or a ship exploding in the atmosphere. It was difficult to tell. He wondered if Isaa was on one of the ships in the rear, grafting on new limbs. He thought about giving the apple to the lieutenant. He may as well get used to the numbness and visions they brought his people. Isaa had laughed and called it shit-faced drunk.

The humans would land soon. They would cut down the ancient orchards of the Highlands and plant apples in the soil. The young of his planet will eat them and become numb. The humans would make them learn an Earth language, probably English. Their priests would try to drive away the old gods and replace them with a singular God who was said to be both cruel and kind.

A small piece of burning metal hit the edge of their shield causing it to crackle. But still the shield held.

"I'll teach you that Earth song if you like." There was nothing better to do, and they might as well begin to learn the language. He only remembered half the words, though the tune had been lodged in his brain for days. "Private Perks went a-marching into Flanders, with his smile, his funny smile. He was lov'd by the privates and commanders, for his smile, his funny smile."

A KNIGHT IN THE ROYAL ARMS

Charity Tahmaseb

Charity Tahmaseb *has slung corn on the cob for Green Giant and jumped out of airplanes (but not at the same time). She's worn both Girl Scout and Army green. These days, she writes fiction and works as a technical writer. Her short speculative fiction has appeared in* Deep Magic, Flash Fiction Online, *and* Cicada.

$\mathcal{A}$ Knight in the Royal Arms

The lobby of the Royal Arms Hotel is so very quiet, and I can taste the hunt in the air. Not that I'd planned on hunting. I only stepped inside out of the rain. Still, the thought tempts me. I don't know what sort of shadow creature lives in this space, but considering the marble floors and gilt-edged mirrors, the prize might be worth the effort.

The glimmer has lulled the concierge to sleep. He slumps over his desk, snores rattling loose paper. The doorman has sunk to the floor. With the sun about to set, that leaves me, the creature, and possibly another tracker as the only ones awake. I take a few steps further in, boots skidding against the marble, not fully committing to the hunt. Not yet.

There *must* be another tracker. Someone must have a claim on this space, and I know I shouldn't venture any farther. But there's no denying DNA, and the shadow creature that resides here is calling to me. So I blow a goodnight kiss to the concierge and find the stairs.

In the third floor hallway, I breathe in dust, fingertips investigating the textured wallpaper. I remain silent and try to gauge whether that creaking floorboard gave me away.

Something always gives me away—a floorboard, the squeaking soles of my boots, a rather clumsy entrance that involves breaking glass. That's all fine when I'm prepared to hunt. Tonight I only wanted a peek.

Behind me, something rasps, brief and brisk, like sandpaper against skin. Mist fills the far end of the corridor, swallowing the glow from the sconces. I squint, but the shadow creature hasn't reached its full, solid form. For this, I am grateful. I race, carving a zigzag path along the corridor. I rattle one doorknob, then another, all of them locked.

At this point, the creature is still mostly vapour. You could poke your fingers through it. But then, you can poke your fingers through a thundercloud. That doesn't make the lightening less deadly.

I sprint down the hall, intent on the last door. I try the knob, then spin, my back against the textured wallpaper. No stairs, not even a fire exit. That's got to be a code violation. At the end of the hall, strands of gray mist probe tentatively. Something that resembles a claw solidifies and holds its shape long enough to tear a hole in the carpet.

Frantic, I try the door one last time. Three things happen. The creature surges forward, filling the hallway with its girth, the door flies open, and I tumble inside. I kick the door shut, my boots and the creature simultaneously slamming against the wood. The door frame shakes but stays put.

The room is dark, curtains drawn. My own ragged breathing fills the space, as does someone else's. I'm staggering to my feet when the lights blaze on. I flinch, cover my eyes with one hand, and attempt to protect myself with the other.

"What the hell?" a voice says.

And then I know: I'm really in trouble.

I grope for a chair and whirl it so it becomes both a shield and a weapon.

"I was here first," the voice says. The tone is strong, authoritative, but a hint of fear invades the arrogance. We all carry that in our voice, those of us who hunt. You can't touch the shadows without them touching you.

"Says who?" I counter. True, I hadn't planned on hunting tonight. Now that I'm here? Why let the opportunity slip by?

"Luke Milner," he says. "Tracker number 1 2 7."

"I know who you are." Or at least *what* he is. There are so few of us that we know each other by reputation, if not by name and face.

"I've been tracking this creature for weeks," he says. "It's on record, claim 5 8 6 7. Feel free to check."

"Oh, I will." I roll my eyes.

"Plus, you totally fell in here." He shakes his head. "You don't even know your way around."

I grip the chair harder. "Oh, sure," I say. "I fell in here. I also flushed out the creature. In what? Less than an hour? How long have you been tracking it again?" I make my voice go all sweet, which is perfectly awful of me. But I can't help it. I dislike most other trackers. Like I said before, it's in my DNA. As a damsel in distress, I have good reason not to like or trust nearly everyone.

"Know the way back out?" Here, Luke Milner offers up a perfectly awful grin, providing me with yet another reason for my aversion.

While logic dictates that if you can find your way in, you can certainly find your way back out again, shadow creatures have a way of erasing that sort of logic. I do have a knack for flushing them out — and an annoying knack for getting stuck in various labyrinths for days. Normally I don't go in without a plan and a week's worth of supplies. The hotel room is covered with that same velvet wallpaper as the hall, all fleurs-de-lis and scrollwork, which makes the space feel elegant despite the freeze-dried meals and canned goods that line the dresser. Luke even has an adorable little camp stove. Plus that queen-size bed? Big enough for two. Not a bad setup, and I can't help but be a little impressed.

He waves his hands as if he can halt both my gaze and my thoughts. "Oh, no. Don't even think about it. My claim. My creature."

"Which you can't seem to flush," I remind him.

The trashcan overflows with wrappers and bottles. A room service tray holds a pot of coffee and pitcher of cream. One whiff tells me it's starting to turn. He's been here for a while without any luck. It's hard to catch a shadow creature on your own; it's even harder to trust another tracker. He can't leave the hotel without risking a claim jumper. But why stay if you can't draw out the creature to begin with?

"You saw it then?" he asks.

"Claws. Sharp. Not sure what it is, but it's big." I shrug. "Maybe a dragon."

He pauses as if considering this — and me. "What makes you so special, then?"

It's a fair if somewhat passive-aggressive question. "I come from a long line of damsels in distress."

Luke snorts.

"Shall I step into the hall and demonstrate?" I gesture toward the door. All hunts require bait. Usually, that's me. I survey the room again. This Luke Milner doesn't seem to have anything that resembles bait.

"You don't look like a damsel in distress."

True. I keep my feet in boots. You try running around in satin slippers or high heels. Tulle and lace and all the rest? Highly flammable, especially in the case of dragons.

"It's in the blood," I say. "Did I not fall in here exactly when I needed to?"

"I was opening the door."

"See? You must have some latent knight-in-shining-armour blood running through your veins."

Luke makes a face.

Okay, *very* latent. But it's there. He's too well-stocked and prepared to be anything else. In theory, I should like that in anyone. Plus, he has that knight-in-shining-armour *look*, wavy hair and features chiselled in all the right places. His eyes might glint with humour if he weren't so surly. Something tells me Luke Milner is often surly.

I've never had any luck with knights in shining armour. They're always too little, too late, and I always end up bound ankle and wrist, eyebrows singed.

Luke narrows his eyes to slits. I cross my arms over my chest, prepared to wait him out. He glances away, but in the mirror, I catch his reflection—all sour milk and resignation.

"Do you have a name?" he says at last, "or do they just call you CJ?"

"C ... J?"

His smirk provides the answer. CJ. *Claim Jumper.*

"I'm Posey Trombelle," I say, putting some teeth into my name. "Tracker number 2 7 8."

"Posey?" He makes another face.

"It's short for Poinsettia. I was a Christmas baby."

His expression goes blank. When he doesn't respond, I add, "My sister was born in February, on the fourteenth. Trust me, she got it worse."

"Well, what do you suggest we do ... Posey?"

"What were you about to do when I fell into your room?"

"Go out," he says. "Reconnaissance."

I raise an eyebrow. Because that? Fairly obvious.

Luke rubs his hands across his face. A growl begins in his throat, but the sound is all frustration without any bite. "I have a theory," he says, "that there's more treasure to be had by not slaying the creature—

"Because most of it is in the lair," I finish.

Oh, of course! How clever. Once you slay the creature, access to any treasure in its lair vanishes. I can't help it. I like the way he thinks. Maybe this Luke has more knight in him than his sour-milk expression suggests.

"You figure out how to do that," I tell him, "and they'll have to call you Sir Luke."

Luke stares at the document on the coffee table, pen clutched in his hand.

"You can't do this without me," I point out.

His knuckles go white.

Granted, a handwritten agreement on hotel stationary pales when compared to a notarized contract. Under the circumstances?

"In fact," I say, tapping three paragraphs down on the paper, "you can't get a better deal than this."

No one would intentionally draw a creature to them, but I've signed on to do just that. Of course, I'm uniquely suited for the task. But while Luke searches out the lair, I must fend off the creature. While I often find myself in precarious situations, I seldom walk into them of my own volition. At least not while leaving myself wide open for betrayal. I occupy the creature, and he runs off with the treasure. I try not to think about that scenario too much.

At last his grip loosens on the pen. He scrawls his name across the bottom of the page, nearly obliterating my own.

Next comes a grappling hook and some rope, which Luke secures at my waist. He threads a whistle onto a length of nylon cord. He ties the ends and then places the whistle around my neck.

"Last resort," he says. "If you need me —— "

"Just blow?"

He cringes. An angry flush covers his cheeks. Before he can turn away, I touch his arm. "Hang on."

From the depths of my cargo pants pocket, I pull a bandana. "A knight shouldn't venture out without a token," I say and tie it around his arm. As tokens go, one-hundred-percent cotton is no substitute for silk, lace, and embroidery. However, the bandana *is* pink.

"Seriously?" Luke eyes the bandana. His fingers twitch over the knot like he might undo the whole thing and toss it on the floor. Instead, he presses his palm against his jeans and sighs.

"See if it doesn't bring you luck," I say.

"I don't believe in luck."

"You should." I give him a two-finger salute and slip out the door.

I take soft steps down the hallway, retracing my original path. I even zigzag, fingertips brushing the textured wallpaper on one side of the corridor and then the next. The ventilation system breathes to life, its steady, mechanical hum the only other sound.

At the corner, I pause. Things are too empty, too quiet. The space around me feels thin, like something else is using up all the available oxygen. Something large. The elevator lobby is the perfect place for an ambush. At least, it's where I'd set one up.

The marble floors in front of the elevator sport a faux Persian rug, a Queen Anne side table, and chairs upholstered in the most amazing shade of canary yellow. The space is pristine. I sniff the air. No lingering scent of sulphur, no rot. What about some slime, a tuft of fur, or even a scale on the floor? Nothing? I taste the air one last time, not trusting this good fortune, but my feet are already moving. To hesitate is to lose this chance.

I rush to the elevators, push the up and down buttons, then retreat to the safety of the stairs.

No sensible tracker uses the elevator—not if they can help it. It's the equivalent of stepping into a lunchbox. Still, it's a handy ruse. A damsel in distress inside an elevator? There's no better bait.

The elevator bell chimes. The doors whoosh open. Dark mist spills out, and a roar echoes against the walls, the sound hearty. The creature must be on the verge of transforming into something solid—and deadly. I'm half a step inside the stairwell when mist curls around the handrail and engulfs my fingers. I glance at the gleaming claws clicking against the lobby floor, then behind me to the creature forming on the stairs.

Here be dragons. Not one, but two. And here I am, right between them.

I cast my gaze upward, searching for a handhold, a window or vent to crawl through ... or that chandelier.

The elevator doors start to close, then spring open again. The creatures are solid enough to trigger elevator doors, not to mention claw, bite, and chomp. They are certainly solid enough to do a damsel-in-distress grab-and-dash.

You know, the usual.

With a hand on the grappling hook, I squint at the chandelier. Will it come crashing down on me mid-swing, effectively doing all the bone-crushing work for the dragons? Steam fills the elevator lobby area. The dragons won't risk a full blast and burn themselves out of their playground. But a stream of fire in my direction?

I don't wait to find out. I swing the grappling hook up and over the chandelier's arms. Light bulbs shatter. I tug. Cracks appear along the ceiling. Plaster dust floats down, fogging the air and coating the floor, the table, the dragon. Before I can swing, a great sucking comes from the elevator — a wind tunnel drawing me in. I grip the rope and brace my feet against the floor. Then the winds reverse.

The explosion of sound startles me. No heat. No fire. Just slime.

"Gesundheit," I say and swing up and over the sniffling dragon.

I land in the hallway, carpet soaking up the sound of my boots. Iridescent dragon snot speckles the textured wallpaper and coats the toes of my boots. I yank the rope one last time. The entire chandelier and half the ceiling crash to the floor. I sprint around the corner to avoid ricocheting debris. Even so,

I choke on dust. My eyes water. I blink fast and hard, taste the grit against my lips. At the end of the hallway, a door flies open.

Luke sticks his head out. "What the hell?"

I give him a little finger wave and run.

Only underwater lamps light the pool area, bathing everything in a liquid blue. My boots squish against damp tile. Moist air clings to my face, turning the plaster dust into muck. With my back to the wall, I ease the lifesaving pole from its bracket. Since Luke's grappling hook is now part of the third floor decor, I need *something*—a tool, a weapon. I test its weight against my palm. Light but strong. It will do.

Now that I'm here, I have the thankless job of luring both dragons to this spot. That shouldn't be too hard. After all, I'm a damsel in distress. Luring is what I do. I take mincing steps around the pool and coo stupid things like, "Oh, no, I might get my satin slippers all wet."

I've never met a creature yet who could tell the difference between satin slippers and steel-toed boots.

Minutes tick by with nothing but the gentle lap of water and my damp footfalls. This was the plan. We didn't have a backup plan in case the creatures didn't show. I'm a damsel in distress. They *always* show.

Except for now.

I kneel at the pool's edge and rinse the plaster from my face. Perhaps it's the water's chemical cocktail—too much bleach and chlorine—that convinces me, but nothing supernatural ever happens in this particular space.

But if the creatures didn't follow me (and they should have, they really should have—I should be trussed up now, tied to the diving board or cooking in the hot tub), then there's only one other spot they could be: their lair.

Which is where Luke was headed — without any backup plan of his own. Can I intercept him? I glance at my watch. Plenty of time before sunrise. Still enough time to — possibly — save Luke. Without another thought, I sprint past the heated towel rack and lounge chairs and crash into the glass doors separating the pool from the mezzanine.

I push. I pull. I rattle the handles so hard the glass shudders. Then I see a telltale glint on the other side of the doors. A dragon scale. I whirl and face the pool. What will it be? Damsel-in-Distress Stew? Or perhaps Luke is the main course, and I'm dessert.

Panic and chlorine clog my throat. Another way out — there must be one. I slip across damp tiles, careen into the changing room doors. These, too, are locked. I survey the space — the lounge chairs, discarded drink glasses with pink sludge and crushed paper umbrellas, a stack of rumpled towels — and discover a way out.

I find the service elevator behind a screen. Steam hisses and clouds roll through the room, as if the water in the pool is already boiling. I wonder if the dragons plan to serve me *al dente*. As soon as the doors screech open, I jump inside, press every button I can, and realize I'm still clutching the lifesaving pole only when the doors clang shut.

I land in the most obvious spot for a lair, down in the basement. The dank and dark, home to boilers and furnaces and the creatures most everyone else has forgotten. Only in this case, it seems the creatures have forgotten this space. Then again, these are dragons—by their very nature, quirky and particular. In this case, there's a pair. A couple, perhaps?

Oh. A couple. Of course. I push the up button on the elevator. There's no time for stairs. I can only hope I'm right and don't end up as a charbroiled snack. When the doors open, I step inside and select the modern equivalent of the high tower: the penthouse suite.

You'd think, as a damsel in distress, I'd be well acquainted with penthouse suites. Sadly, my luck runs toward trolls and ogres. On the rare occasions I'm captured, I end up in landfills or junkyards or, for the occasional eco-conscious goblins, recycling centres.

The doors open on the penthouse level. Smoke fills the elevator compartment. The acrid scent tickles the back of my throat, and I choke on a cough. I step out and crunch something beneath the sole of my boot. The remains shine in rainbow patterns the way only a dragon scale can.

I take a cautious look around. The glimmer is in full force here. Despite the smoke, I can taste the magic that lets the dragons lie dormant during the day and come out to play at night. They haven't taken over the entire floor, not yet, but the lair is well established.

I creep forward, pole outstretched like a spear, eyes cast downward. The last thing I want is to track through a pile of ash. That can mean only one thing. The tracker community may be combative, but the death of one of our own weighs heavy. My stomach squeezes tight. I clutch the pole harder. I want to close my eyes, because I don't want to see that pile of ash. I keep them open out of fear and respect.

At the end of the hall, I brush fingertips over the penthouse door then press my palm against the panelled wood. Warm, but not searing hot. That's something. Now for a distraction. I need something loud and sure, something these dragons won't miss.

I lean against the wall and that something thumps against my chest. Luke's whistle. I grip it between my teeth and blow with all my might. Then I sprint down the corridor and launch myself behind a settee. The hiding place is flimsy. But once dragons get up a good gallop, they have a difficult time stopping, never mind turning around.

The penthouse door flies open. Claws scrape against the Italian marble floor, leaving wide grooves in its surface. The dragons galumph straight for the elevator, bypassing the settee. I crawl from beneath it, scrabble to gain purchase, then race for the penthouse.

I slam the door. It doesn't matter if the dragons hear. They're too clever to stay fooled for long anyway. Still, I throw the deadbolt for the slight delay it will give me. For good measure, I jam the lifesaving pole behind the handle.

"Luke?" I call out.

A grunt comes from the bedroom. Among satin sheets, rose petals, and candlelight, I find him, all trussed up, bound ankle and wrist, damsel-in-distress style. He grunts again, words muffled by a pink bandana — *my* bandana — gagging his mouth. So much for luck.

I can't help it; I know it's cruel. I laugh.

"You wouldn't happen to have a knife, would you?" he says when I undo the gag, a frown fighting the relief on his face.

"Swiss Army." I slice through the ropes around his wrists and set to work on his ankles.

A crash reverberates through the entire penthouse. My hands

shake and the blade skitters up and over the rope, but it only catches on Luke's jeans. A whoosh fills the air, followed by the cheerful crackle of burning wood.

"We have all of three seconds," Luke says.

In those three seconds, I hack away the last of the rope. Luke smashes the window with a chair. He secures a grappling hook (one covered with plaster dust) and swings us — me clutched in one arm — out the window, past jagged glass, and over the ledge.

We land one story below, breezing through an already-opened window. When our feet touch ground, Luke releases me. I tumble into yet another canary yellow chair, knocking it over. I suck in air free of smoke, grateful for the hard floor that has just bruised my hip bones. As landings go, this one wasn't half-bad. I catch Luke's eye and point to the window.

"I like to go in with a back-up plan," he says.

An admirable quality for a knight in shining armour.

"You're pretty handy with a knife," he adds.

"You're not bad with ropes."

The building trembles. Plaster rains down, dusting my skin — again. The elevator doors pop open and shut.

"We should leave," I say. "They'll destroy everything just to get to us."

Even their own playground. Threat to their treasure brings out the nasty side of shadow creatures.

To my surprise, Luke takes my hand to help me up. He keeps a grip on it during our entire flight down the stairs. Even outside, with the first rays of sun banishing the night, he doesn't let go. He pulls us forward, intent on getting us away, while I scan the structure.

"All clear?" he asks.

"Looks that way. For now."

Four blocks from the hotel, we slow our steps. I keep the vigil, always tossing a quick glance behind. With the rising sun, the glimmer loosens its hold. The dragons will return to mist and shadows. The hotel will right itself before any of the regular guests can notice anything amiss. Already, glass in the smashed windows has repaired itself.

"I never thought to look in the penthouse until you came along," Luke says.

I inspire thoughts of the penthouse? Is this a good thing?

"The living room was the treasure trove, but I decided to check the bedroom before leaving," he continues. "I walked in on them while they were ... I mean, he was ...

"Entertaining a special lady friend?" I supply.

A flush washes across his cheekbones—a hint of pink to match the sunrise. It's kind of adorable.

"Yeah." He clears his throat. "That."

Luke pulls a small velvet sack from his shirt. "By our contract." He tips the bag and coins flow into his palm. "Fifty-fifty split. You earned it."

"So did you."

"It wasn't all bad," he says, "working with you."

Is that a compliment? I peer at him, intrigued. "Well, you *are* good with ropes," I say. "And I don't loathe you like I do most knights in shining armour."

He tosses the coins in the air and catches them neatly again. "When was the last time you earned a haul like this?"

Almost never. Damsels in distress always get the short end of things, even when we're the ones who make things happen. I can't count the number of times my fellow trackers have left me bound, wrist and ankle, and made off with the treasure. Even though my boots are singed and snot covered, my hair a plaster-streaked mess, this time, the prize was worth it. This time, I had a worthy partner.

"There's a lot more where this came from." Luke stares hard just past my shoulder, like the only way he can say this is to not look at me. "We could spend days, weeks, and still not find it all."

We? "So you're not reporting me as a claim jumper?"

His lips twitch. "Well, you know, I can't seem to flush them on my own."

"That's my specialty."

"We'd need a contract."

I nod toward a diner at the end of the block. They serve a huge breakfast special—eggs over easy, sizzling bacon, pancakes drenched in maple syrup—the perfect meal after a night of successful tracking.

"Everyone knows a contract written on the back of a paper placemat is totally binding," I say. "We could talk about it. Maybe over some coffee?"

The sun crests the hotel, casting the street in a glow to rival the canary yellow furniture, banishing the creatures to shadow for another day. We turn toward the diner. Luke tosses the coins and lets them fall into his hand one last time.

"Maybe we should," he says.

THE HAIR IN THE BAG

Jenny Blackford

Jenny Blackford *is a poet and author based in Newcastle, Australia. Her poems have appeared in* The Pedestal Magazine, Strange Horizons, Star*Line *and* Rhysling *anthologies, as well as various anthologies and venerable literary journals. Pamela Sargent called her subversively feminist historical novella set in ancient Greece,* The Priestess and the Slave, *"elegant." Her first poetry chapbook,* The Duties of a Cat, *was published in* 2013 *by Pitt Street Poetry.*

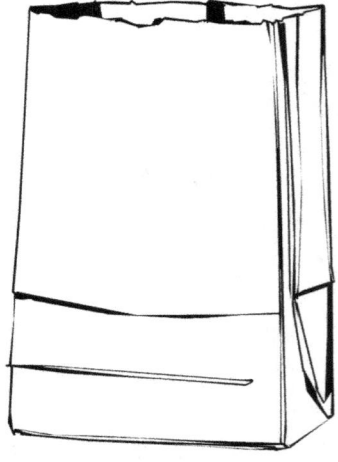

The Hair in the Bag

She keeps her hair in a drugstore bag
in the boot of the small pink car.
We all get shown it.

Or perhaps it crawls on its curled blonde tendrils,
silent as the thin grey cat that shadows her.
We all get shown it.

The nurses don't believe her, but see the smoky creature
there under her chair, toying with one golden strand.
Where will it go,

when there's no hair left on the pale bone dome?
The plastic bag is two-thirds full of her crowning pride.
We all get shown it.

CANNERY ROW

Susan Pieters

Susan Pieters is a fourth-generation Californian who took warm weather for granted until she moved to Vancouver. Now that she's a Canadian, she sits at home during rainy nights and writes about sunshine. This story, told from the point of view of a young boy, surprised her.

$\mathcal{C}$ANNERY ROW

I adjust the focus on my Dad's Nikon and shoot.

The building is simple bare wood, plain and honest, no cheerful veneer of paint. The horizontal boards are aged from the sun. They've been bleached past silver to dark again. I wonder if a fire has passed and singed the edges into charcoal. But I think it's from the sun, because that's what light does, given enough time. It reveals the scientific truth of a thing and brings it back to elemental earth, to essential carbon, even as it stands.

"That's where Steinbeck wrote *Cannery Row*, right in there." My mother stands beside me as I take the picture. She's lit a cigarette. It's the seventies, and women are entitled to their privileges.

I step away from her. I'm only fourteen, but I'm my father's son, and I don't smoke.

My Dad has a wide-angle lens, and I wish I had it with me. I want to capture how small the two-storey building is next to the tall cannery buildings. The canneries also look decrepit, empty, deserted. Faded lettering on the sides.

My mother gets halfway through her cigarette. "Most people don't know about this place. But it should be a monument."

She nods at the rickety wooden staircase leading to a single wooden door at the top, as if there should be a plaque mounted with Steinbeck's name. She narrows her eyes a bit and blows her smoke up in the air at an angle, the way she does at parties when she's talking to someone important. I suspect she's excited that there's no marker, so she's in on a special secret, a member of some inner circle.

I crank the advance forward to the next number. I turn the camera on my mother. She's got a train of smoke obscuring her face, but I use the f-stop like my Dad showed me and tighten the field onto her hair. She catches me just as I snap it.

I thumb the ratchet again. I have ten shots left on this roll.

Just on the other side of those buildings is the ocean, but we can't see it from here. You can't even hear it. I try to imagine what it would have been like when these canneries were in operation: the noise, the stink. How would a writer get anything done inside a little laboratory building, when next door and all down the street were a million fish being gutted and tinned and loaded up into trucks? Where would Steinbeck go for fresh air?

My mother's about done with her cigarette. "They used to have big parties in there. Those were the days. Did you get a good shot?" She doesn't wait for my answer but drops the glowing butt to the street and twists her shoe on it like she's swinging with a dance partner. "They'll probably tear this all down soon. When you read the book someday, remember I showed you this. Save that picture."

There's money in abalone, now that Monterey Bay has been fished out. We walk a few blocks back along the street and enter a private laboratory where my father has been working all day as a consultant for an abalone farm. The place sounds fancy, but it's not. It's an old converted warehouse with a cement floor filled with small circular tanks designed as watering troughs for cattle. The water tanks are lined with ocean rocks, nurseries for the abalone to grow. It's cool and dim in here like a cave. All around is the sound of dripping seawater as leaking pipes pump in salt water from the ocean twenty feet away. The smell of salt and kelp is stronger inside than it was outside, as if they're bottling up the Pacific like a perfume.

The owner comes from a back corner to greet my mother. I look at the owner, Mr Dubois, carefully. I can't figure out why he looks so different from my Dad. They both wear the same thing, white lab coats and black-framed glasses, but Mr Dubois doesn't look like a scientist. Maybe it's because he has polished shoes, a big smile, and an even tan. He's not Mexican, though. My mother told me his accent was French. Continental French.

"I'll take you over to the professor." Mr Dubois loves to call my dad 'the professor' in front of everyone, even my dad. And Dad does look the part. We walk towards the fluorescent lamps, where he's bent over a workstation table. His glasses aren't much thicker than Mr Dubois's, but when Dad looks up at us I get the feeling he's looking from the other side of a telescope and observing us from another planet. His lab coat has yellowed stains, and there are numerous black streaks at his breast pocket where he keeps his felt tip pens. My mother bought him a protective plastic sheath for his pocket, but he forgets to use it.

Dad looks at my mother, goes "Mmm-hmm," and turns back to write something on the long yellow writing pad where he's taking notes. There are little Petri dishes and grease pencils on the table, and he has a dissection microscope at his elbow. His calculator has been left on, although his slide rule is also in use. He's taught me to use both, but I'm not allowed to use them on my homework assignments.

Mr Dubois places his hand on my mother's elbow and turns her towards a back room. "We might be a while yet," he says apologetically. He turns on the hot plate to make some coffee for my mother. He reaches in the fridge. Stashed between glass jars of floating specimens, there are cans of beer. He hands me a Coke.

The camera is hanging around my neck, but I've been told not to use it inside the lab. There are too many secrets, my mom said. There's a lot of money in abalone, because there are a lot of risks. Apparently Mr Dubois has taken out a very large loan to start this business, and he's offered to pay my dad in shares if he can solve the problems. Several local ventures have started up, hoping to get rich. Each one has hired a different specialist. Mr Dubois is already ahead of the competition, because Dad has figured out how to get the abalone to reproduce. The problem now is that the larva, called veliger, won't 'settle': they float in the water but won't stick to the rocks and grow.

My mother accepts her cup of coffee. "Don't worry, Maurice, he'll figure it out. He always does."

My dad is a small potatoes professor at an underfunded college, but everyone says he's 'got a way with critters'. Dad's not as good with people, or committees, and he swears when he gets home after a meeting, but when it comes to keeping his marine collections alive, he always finds a way.

We drive to Carmel to spend the night at Mr Dubois's house. It's a short ride, but as we go up the hill, even a fourteen-year-old kid can smell the money in the air. The trees grow over the road and ferns show up like we're in a terrarium. The cars are freshly waxed and the house numbers are hand-carved wood. We turn at a funny angle up a private road.

Mr Dubois is divorced, but his son Benny lives with him. He's thirteen, so all the adults assume we will be great friends and stay out of the way until dinner time. Benny leads me down the hillside towards a tree fort.

"Why'd you bring that camera?" Benny climbs up the ladder faster than I do, since he has no encumbrance. "Is that yours?"

"It's my dad's." I snap the leather cover off so he can see the top, the Nikon logo. "But he trusts me with it."

It's already getting dark, and I hear a few creaking peals of frogs from scattered places in the hillside. They're like orchestra players warming up their instruments with off-sounding notes. I take the camera and take a picture of the tree branches against the sunset, wishing I could record the sound.

Benny consults his watch, a water-resistant Timex like Dad wears. It looks too big on his wrist. "Let's go back for dinner."

The barbecue is ready for the steaks. Benny and I are hungry, but the grown-ups aren't in a hurry because they're all drinking beer. They don't talk much. My dad still hasn't solved the settling problem.

Mr Dubois ruffles his son's hair. "Did you play Dennis the Menace?"

Benny gives me a look. He takes his father's hand and tugs a little, as if he wants to tell him something private. Mr Dubois takes two steps towards the pool, and Benny pushes him in.

There's a big splash, the kind that echoes. My mother holds her beer in the air so it won't get water inside. My father glares so Benny doesn't get encouraged to do it again on somebody else. Mr Dubois sputters up and grabs the edge of the pool. His lips are smiling but his eyes are looking for Benny with intent. His glasses are missing.

My mother steps over to give Mr Dubois a hand up out of the pool and leans too far over. We all see it coming.

When she splashes in herself, even my father laughs. My mother rises to the surface but doesn't come back to the edge right away. She floats on her back, her dress wafting around her legs like a jellyfish. Even Benny is riveted.

My father honours the festivities with a pun. "I see you were serious about pooling our talents, Maurice."

Mr Dubois winces. My mother does a side-kick. "Don't encourage him."

That's exactly the recognition my father is looking for. He lifts his beer can. "I can honestly say your hops-pitality is ..." My Dad stares into the pool at the beer can submerged under the water, peeing its golden liquid. "It's the *yeast*."

I twist the black cover off the lens of my Dad's Nikon. I was thinking about the scene in the pool, but now what I really want is a photo of my father's face. He's got eureka written all over him, and he's pawing at his breast pocket for a pen that isn't there. I don't have a flash, but I snap a shot before he goes inside the house.

My mother turns her wet head to Mr Dubois. "What's beer got to do with abalone?" As she twists around in the pool, her skirt circles around her, but the fabric around her chest melts tight.

Benny taps me on the shoulder. It's fair warning, and I put the camera down safely before he grabs me. I manage to get him to fall into the pool first, but I follow at his heels. It's warm, and my tennis shoes kick against the sinking beer can.

"I think the professor is telling us we're going to be rich," Mr Dubois comments, loosening his ruined tie. "Benny, please dive for my glasses."

Mr Dubois was wrong. My dad cracked the mystery, but a month later, there's been a breakthrough at a big university, and a research professor with a team of graduate students has documented the secrets of settling abalone larva and published it for all the world to see.

Dad no longer goes up to Monterey. He turns the guest bathroom into a darkroom and teaches me how to develop film.

We huddle together with the orange light bulb on, inhaling the smell of warm chemicals like we're cooking soup. We process the roll from Monterey, and he puts it into the enlarger.

My father stands back. "Here, I should let you do this."

I adjust an image of the dark building on Cannery Row, but the edges of the building are too rough, the boards blurry no matter what I do. I thought I'd stood still, but maybe I'd moved.

My Dad leans in closer. "That's the old Pacific Biological labs, where Ed Ricketts worked. He wrote *Between Pacific Tides*. Too bad it's not a sharp picture, you got a good angle on this."

The next one is of my mother. Her eyes remind me of a cat. My father doesn't say anything.

I scroll past pictures of the tree branches. They look empty without the sound of frogs. "Benny told me he threw frogs from the tree fort."

My Dad just shakes his head.

I pause on the picture of my father's retreating back after his eureka moment. I go on to the last picture, adjusting the focus so it's sharp on the two people sitting together. My mother's hair is still wet. Then I quickly turn the knob to blur it. I'd forgotten about that picture. I'd taken it when I was supposed to be in bed, when my father was up late working on his eureka theory.

My father reaches out to his hand to stop me. Turns my hand so the picture comes true. He peers through his black-framed glasses, the ones that can see things from another planet.

"Don't ever hide from what you see, son." He puts his hand on my shoulder. "It's a scientist's job to find out the truth of things, even when we don't like what we find."

We turn back to the first photograph of Cannery Row. He's not talkative any more. He lets me cut the photographic paper myself, set the timer, and dip the exposed paper into the chemicals.

The building and its silvery black boards emerge from the empty paper like a ghost becoming visible. My mother's smoke was drifting across my lens, which is why the picture isn't clear.

I hold the paper in the solution too long, because I keep thinking that there is more to this picture that hasn't appeared yet. I keep looking on those stairs, where the smoke is drifting, because I know that the steps leading up to the door are not empty at all. There's a writer there with his elbows on his knees as he takes a drag and looks out over the street. I'm not sure if it's Steinbeck or Ricketts. He's avoiding taking up his pen. He's giving himself just a few more minutes before he goes back inside with his very heavy burden of human and scientific truth.

THE POOL GUY

Adam Golub

Adam Golub *is an American Studies professor who teaches courses on literature, childhood, popular culture, and monsters at California State University, Fullerton. His stories have appeared in* The Bookends Review, 101 Fiction, The Sirens Call, *and* Winamop. *He is co-editor of* Monsters in the Classroom: Essays on Teaching What Scares Us, *(McFarland, 2017). 'The Pool Guy' was Brenda Carre's choice as first runner up in our 2016 Raven Short Story Contest and earned honourable mention in the 38th New Millennium Writings Award for Fiction. Adam lives in Fullerton, CA.*

THE POOL GUY

Ty took a break from sexting Maddie to ask the pool guy about the leaf blower guy.

"I heard someone attacked him with a golf club," said Ty.

"That's right," said the pool guy. "Someone just walked up and cracked him, *Goodfellas* style. Jesús tried to fight back with the leaf blower, and supposedly there was a duel for a few seconds, all King Arthur and shit, but police say this maniac was on a mission, he was hulking, all Rage-Virused out. Jesús never stood a chance. He's got a skull fracture, man. Lacerations on his arms. Teeth are all busted up."

"That's terrible," Ty said as his phone chimed.

And then I climb on top of you like a jockey on his favourite horse.

Maddie was a simile sexter.

"Lonnie in eighteen has a get well card clipped to his door that we're all signing," said the pool guy as he skimmed his net along the surface by the deep end. "He'll bring it to the hospital tomorrow."

"Cool," said Ty.

Nice, he texted Maddie.

"Hey, I've noticed some ducks have been hanging out in the pool lately. You finding any duck shit in there?" asked Ty.

"Ducks? What, they take a wrong turn on the way to the Sopranos? I haven't noticed any duck waste, but don't worry, the chemicals will kill off anything in there. I mean dissolve it completely, *Alien* acid style. Duck crap don't stand a chance in this pool."

"I know where I'll be taking all my shits from now on," said Ty.

"How *Caddyshack* of you, Mr K," said the pool guy.

"Cinderella story. Outta nowhere," Ty said, looking down at his phone.

I grind on you like coffee beans making sweet hot coffee.

Maddie worked in a Starbucks.

"Speaking of Cinderella story, how's the screenplay coming along?" asked the pool guy.

"Sequels are hard."

That's it, texted Ty. *Make mine a grande.*

"I've got a million-dollar idea for a movie," said the pool guy. "You wanna hear it? I can tell you, but then I'd have to kill you."

"I'll take my chances."

"It's about a guy who cleans pools."

"Shocker."

"One day he shows up at one of his regular jobs and finds a body floating in the pool. Flips him over, pulls him out. It's no one he recognizes. Turns out nobody knows who this floater is. No ID, no one files a missing persons report. It's a complete mystery. Cops don't really care because they have enough on their plate, so they don't launch an investigation. Death is ruled a John Doe suicide. So the pool guy makes a point to try to discover this man's identity. The deeper he digs, the more questions he asks, the more obsessed he gets. But it's dead ends all around. No one knows who this guy is.

"The pool guy's got a blurry photo of the floater that he took with his phone the day he found him, and he keeps a print copy of the photo on his bathroom mirror. Gradually the face in the photo starts coming into focus. Like, each day he wakes up and looks at the picture on the mirror and the face is a little more defined, more recognizable. Until the pool guy realizes that the body floating in the pool is him. *He's the dead guy.* He found his own body. But he also discovers that it wasn't suicide, it was murder. And then it becomes a race against time to figure out who killed him, because each day that the photo on the mirror becomes clearer, the pool guy starts to fade. Like in real life, his body starts kinda disappearing. And just when he's on the verge of solving the mystery, just as he's on the track of the killer, he gets hit by a bus, because he's almost invisible at that point and the bus driver can't see him crossing the street."

"But where are the ducks?" asked Ty. "What this screenplay needs is more ducks."

"You dig it? It's like *The Sixth Sense* meets *DOA*."

"Meets Dorian Grey."

"What?" asked the pool guy. "Who?"

I want you to explode like a baking soda volcano.

Maddie was working on her multiple subject teaching credential at Cal State Northridge.

"If you don't like that one, I've got one more," said the pool guy. "A million-dollar idea for a documentary. Wanna hear it?"

"Fire away," said Ty.

"You track down as many guys as you can who are named Elliott who were kids when *E.T. the Extraterrestrial* was in the movie theatres, and you ask them what it was like to grow up as *Ell-ee-ot*. Like, how badly were they teased? How annoying was it? How did it shape who they were? Did they change their names? Go by a nickname instead? Or did they embrace it, introduce themselves to people in the E.T. voice, have girls say their name like that in bed? It'd be awesome to see all these Elliotts interviewed in one movie."

"My brother's name is Elliott," said Ty.

"Sweet. We can start with him."

"He lives in Kyoto."

"Even better. We can ask him if the Chinese do the E.T. voice with him."

"Japan. Japanese."

"Sweet. *Lost in Translation*. Is your brother like Bill Murray?"

I want to be inside you like E.T. wants to go home, Ty texted.

???? replied Maddie.

"My brother moved to Japan eight years ago. He started off teaching English, but now he's a male escort. He accompanies lonely Japanese women on dates. Sometimes he has sex with them. Sometimes he kisses them. Mostly he just holds their hand or dances with them."

The pool guy stopped skimming and looked at Ty. "For real?"

"Totally."

"I need to move to China."

"I tease him all the time."

"About being an escort?"

"No. I say his name in the E.T. voice. I also send him texts and emails that say, 'phone home.'"

"How does he feel about that?"

"You should ask him. He's coming to visit next week. Hasn't

been in the States for five years. Last time he came back was for my dad's funeral. He gave a bizarre eulogy. Something about dad being like an ancient garden, a perfect arrangement of rocks, and Elliott's job as a son had been to sweep debris away from the rocks, to keep the rocks pristine. Apparently in Japan there's a guy whose job it is to sweep the rocks at the temple. My brother said he was the flower keeper and dad was the temple garden. Flower keeper? No one knew what he was talking about."

Ty suddenly remembered winning a tackle box in a father-son fishing contest when he was seven. His dad had hooked the fish, but Ty reeled it in.

"During that visit Elliott started smoking again," he continued. "He had quit before moving to Japan. Which was hard because everyone in Japan smokes. So after the funeral he went back to Japan and as far as I know he's still smoking."

"Well, there's no smoking by the pool, Mr K., if you take your brother out here. I'm sure you know that. Technically no alcohol either, but no one's going to ask you to open your Thermos, if you know what I mean."

Ty snapped his fingers and pointed at the pool guy. "You wanna sip?" He held up his Thermos.

"Thanks, but I'm on the clock. I don't drink on the job. Just get high."

"You high now?"

"I don't toke and tell."

I want to suck you like a Dyson vacuum, texted Maddie.

Maddie asked for a Dyson for Christmas last year but Ty took her to Temecula instead.

"By the way, why do you think Jesús was attacked? Do they have any leads on the guy?" asked Ty.

"No suspects yet. Just a description. Some white guy in a baseball cap. It was probably leaf blower rage, man. It's a thing now. People can't deal with the noise and they just lose it. I've talked to a couple leaf blowers who say they live in fear every day. Imagine going to work worried someone's going to pound on you just for doing your job?"

"Well, leaf blowers are really annoying," said Ty as he texted *vroom* to Maddie.

"So annoying that you'd be willing to kill?" asked the pool guy.

"I think I'm more inclined to experience pool guy rage. All of this, 'Don't go in the water for five minutes, I just put some chemicals in there.' Makes me crazy. Makes me want to put the net over your head and choke you and drown you."

"Ease up, Hannibal Lecter."

"Do you still hear the screaming of the lambs, Clarice?" asked Ty.

The pool guy chuckled and went back to skimming. "Why is your brother coming to visit this time? Someone else die?" he asked.

"My mom's getting remarried," said Ty.

"It's like *Four Weddings and a Funeral.*"

"Well, more like one funeral and a wedding, but yeah."

"How do you feel about the guy your mom's marrying?"

"He owns a dog pool. You two would get along."

"What's a dog pool?"

"It's like a dog park but it's a pool. People take their dogs over to his house and he's got a special pool in his backyard for dogs. It's shaped like a bone. He even offers swimming lessons for the dogs."

"Does he teach them the doggie paddle?" The pool guy guffawed.

"Rich people pay to bring their dogs there. The dogs swim while the owners sit around the pool and sip margaritas and talk about investment opportunities."

"Does he need a pool guy?"

"He lives in Houston."

Ty's phone chimed again: *You're gonna give me a big O like a crop circle.*

Maddie grew up in Ackley, Iowa.

Phone home, texted Ty.

??? replied Maddie. *Did my mom call you or something?*

"His name is Dan Kleon," said Ty. "I only met him once. I had barbecue with him in Seal Beach. He was in town for the weekend. My mother wanted us to go out to dinner together. To bond. To earn one another's approval, as she put it. He spent the entire meal telling me how he had recently erased his identity from the Internet. He'd hired a company that scrubs every mention of you from cyberspace. They essentially make you unsearchable. The virtual *you* becomes forgotten. I wondered why this guy felt the need to erase himself. What had he done? What was in his past that he wanted forgotten? What was he hiding?

"I asked these questions to his face and he told me he just wanted his privacy back. He was willing to pay top dollar for it. There were no skeletons in his closet, he said. In fact, he told me, my mother was contemplating hiring the same company. InterPurge is their name, although you can't find them with any search engine. Apparently InterPurge is an elite operation that works through word of mouth. You can only secure a consultation with them if one of their clients refers you. And the referral must be made in person. No email, no letter, no phone call. It was worth every dime, he told me, because now no one will ever find him online. But what about your business, the dog pond, I asked. How do customers find you? And you know what he said?"

"What did he say?" asked the pool guy.

"Yellow pages. Dude advertises in the yellow pages. In the phone book. But his name doesn't appear in the ad. Just the name of his business. And you know what the business is called?"

"What's it called?" asked the pool guy.

"The Pooch Pond. My new stepfather owns and operates The Pooch Pond. This is my mom's husband-to-be."

The pool guy was on his knees pouring chemicals into the skimmer basket by the side of the pool.

"You want me to help you kill him, *Fargo* style?" he asked.

"I just want so badly for this guy to be full of shit," said Ty. "Like that pool."

The pool guy stood up and dried his hands on the small orange towel hanging from his belt.

"Listen, you need to wait five or ten minutes before you go in the water. I just put some chemicals in there," he said.

"Whatever," said Ty.

The pool guy reminded Ty about Lonnie's card for Jesús. Then the two said their goodbyes.

I'm wet like a handy wipe before it's exposed to too much air, texted Maddie.

The gate clacked loudly as the pool guy walked away, the long net slung over his shoulder.

Whatever, texted Ty, before he erased the entire message thread from his phone and followed the pool guy to his truck.

INGLEWOOD COURTS, EDMONTON

Benjamin Hertwig

Benjamin Hertwig's writing has appeared or is forthcoming in the New York Times, the Literary Review of Canada, Prairie Fire, Pleiades, THIS, Freefall, Matrix, QWERTY, Sugar House Review, Maine Review, and Word Riot. His debut book of poems, Slow War, is coming out with McGill-Queen's in 2017.

Inglewood Courts, Edmonton

Zane was sixteen, moved
to Canada from Croatia, was good
at basketball and said he was coming
right back. Stay at the court, he said,
and tell the girls I'll return in a bit if
they come to say hi. Zane was older
than you and shirtless. You became
angry after an hour and shot the ball
like he was watching: every swish tore
a hole in his lie. He wasn't coming
back. So you walked away too.
The grass in the field was long and fit
for cows, the asphalt perspiring like a can
of cold Pepsi, streetlights beside the dying
mall flickered beatifically when you ordered
a holy burger and prayed to something
on the way home — hands cloying
with sweat, wishing you had someone
to lie to, that Zane knew something
you didn't: no one comes to that court
after dark.

THE BUMBLEBEE FLASH FICTION CONTEST

THE BUMBLEBEE FLASH FICTION CONTEST

The Bumblebee Flash Fiction Contest: a call for short, sassy, sweet, and stinging fiction of no more than 750 words. That call was answered with an abundance of polished stories, almost an embarrassment of riches from those most diligent of busy-bee craftspersons, authors. This issue publishes both the Bumblebee winner, 'Crushed Velvet' by Ingrid Jendrzejewski, and the runner-up, Jay Allisan's 'Kiss Kiss Bang Bang'.

Judge Bob Thurber says of 'Crushed Velvet': *Among its merits are its playful, whimsical tone. Its seductive smoothness. Its refreshing eccentricity and, of course, its good fashion sense.*

'Kiss Kiss Bang Bang' received his nod *for its jaunty seriousness and obvious merit.*

The other eight shortlisted stories were 'Lucky' by Charity Tahmaseb, 'The Pit' by Katie Gray, 'The Weight of Time' by Leslie Wibberley, 'Even Steven' by Melanie Cossey, 'The Utility of Mandatory Hilarity' by Soramimi Hanarejima, 'Roshan' by Tristan Marajh, and 'Bedside' by William Kaufmann.

Congratulations to Ingrid, Jay, and the shortlisted authors, and thanks to all our contest entrants who made choosing so difficult.

Ingrid Jendrzejewski grew up in Vincennes, Indiana, and studied creative writing at the University of Evansville then physics at the University of Cambridge. She now lives in the UK, where she is trying to get up the nerve to declutter her wardrobe. Links to her work can be found at www.ingridj.com and she occasionally tweets @LunchOnTuesday.

CRUSHED VELVET

BY INGRID JENDRZEJEWSKI

When I get home, my skinny clothes are dancing. They are making a terrific racket.

"What do you think you're doing?" I ask, and the answer comes back all chiffon bubbly from my first prom dress: "Celebrating!"

"Celebrating our freedom!" adds a snarky velvet bustier from my goth phase.

I let its impudent tone slide by unchecked. I don't like mess, but they all look so happy, I decide to join in. When I break into a jaunty jive, I am, for a moment, transported; it's been a long time since I've let loose. But before long, I come to the uncomfortable realization that I am the only one still dancing. My work clothes are clinging to my body, startled and suspicious. I stop dead in my two-step.

"Yes, well," ruffles the lace brassiere in which I lost my virginity, "we'll be off now. We were just waiting until you got home so that we could say goodbye."

My cheeks flush, so I brush my hands briskly over my pantsuit to eliminate creases. "What are you talking about?"

"Oh, come on," pipe the matching lace knickers. "It's no fun being cooped up in drawers and closets for years on end. Even *you* go out once in a while!"

"To *work*," I retort, instantly realizing I'm not helping my cause.

"Yes ..." sneers the Liza Minnelli bowler hat as it bobs knowingly at the Rocky Horror hot pants.

The crop top is more forgiving. "Really, though," it says gently. "You're not going to wear us again, are you now?"

My control-top pantyhose snigger around my waist, tickling my stretch marks. I snap the waistband. "I could. I might!"

"Oh, sweetheart ..." sigh the fishnets, and all of us settle into a long silence.

My eyes sting and the corners of my mouth tremble. But, like any good general, I rally. I scan the room, survey my resources, size up my army. It is time, I decide, to heft my weight.

"Ladies!" I cry, and my current wardrobe — the clothing I've trained up with a harsh regimen of ironing and starch — unfold to attention. I look them over and nod. They aren't pretty, but they can get the job done. "Get 'em!"

Before my skinny clothes know what's happening, my active-duty wardrobe is upon them. It is utter carnage: a veritable massacre of colour and flounce. Muumuus smother slim-fit jeans, elasticized waistbands strangle string bikinis. Ponchos pull no punches. There is one last, desperate rush of sequins as a clutch of evening dresses makes a break for the door, but they are cut off by a phalanx of girdles and reinforced bras. Within minutes, the uprising is crushed like velvet.

When it's over, I stand triumphant amidst the boning and tulle. My work clothes celebrate; the green beret flaps with pride. Together, we string the skinny clothes on hangers, crucify them with clothes pegs. When they've all been put back in place, I shut the closet doors and smile.

The crop top was right. I'm never going to wear those things again. But old clothes hold onto memories forever and know too many secrets. No way am I going to let them give me the slip—not, at least, while my overall satisfaction with things like life, work, and myself remains hanging by a thread.

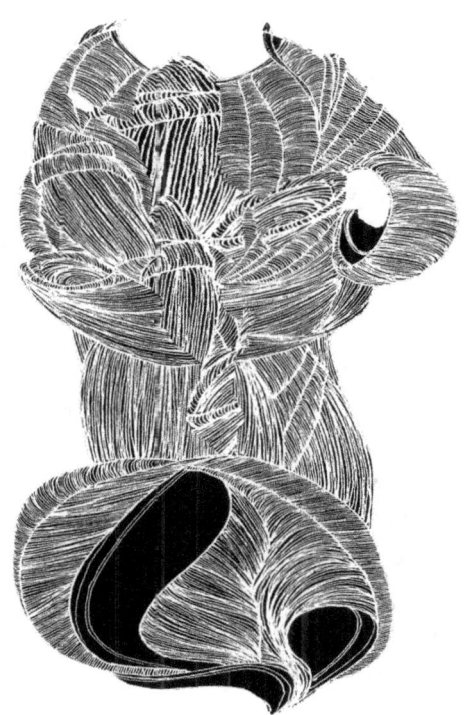

Jay Allisan is part-time author and full-time thinker. She lives in southern Alberta, where she works as a swim coach. Visit her online at www.jayallisan.com.

Kiss Kiss, Bang Bang

BY JAY ALLISAN

It wasn't until grade school that Brody realized the difference between boys and girls. From the outside they looked alike. Girls wore pants. Boys wore pants. Girls had short hair. Boys had short hair. Girls romped through the mud and played with toy trucks and got into fistfights with each other just like the boys, and all the mothers would roll their eyes and say, "Girls will be girls." Brody thought boys and girls were pretty much the same.

Until the first day of grade school, when Sally Conklin from across the street showed him what she got at the girls-only assembly.

"It's a gun," she said proudly. "All the girls got them. Mrs Garfield says we don't get bullets until we're older, but these squirt some kind of slime that makes you itchy. So watch out!" She stuck the gun in her waistband. "What did you get at your assembly?"

"A warning," Brody said. "About how to treat girls."

The warning was starting to make sense.

In middle school Bobby Ziefenberger got shot when he tried to look up Mary-Lou Churchill's dress. She shot him right in the chest, and Bobby plopped down in the dirt and howled until someone ran to get a teacher. All the girls clustered around Mary-Lou and kept their guns pointed at Bobby. All the boys stood back with their hands in their pockets. When Mr Wu got there he asked what happened, and everyone told him the same thing.

"I was just joking!" Bobby whined. "I wasn't hurting her. She didn't have to shoot me!"

Mary-Lou crossed her arms and stuck her tongue out at him. Mr Wu said, "Go see the nurse, Bobby. We'll discuss this after school."

When Bobby was gone, the girls put their guns away and went back to playing. Mr Wu took the boys aside.

"It's not a joke," Mr Wu said quietly. He looked serious but also sad. "Remember that. It could save your life."

"I don't know about saving our lives," George Polk whispered to Brody during math class. "But I bet it could save our moms some laundry."

Brody looked over at Bobby, who had an ice pack strapped to his chest. Bobby's shirt was bright pink from the paint pellet, and his face was even pinker, because everyone was staring. Brody thought that was worst part, having everyone know what you did.

"It's no big deal now," Brody whispered back. "But I hear they get bullets in high school."

§

On junior prom night, Brody picked up his girlfriend, Clarisse. He thought she looked hot. He told her so. His gaze fell to her cleavage, and she waggled a finger at him.

"Careful," she said, patting her clutch. "It's in here. And even though they're made of wax, the bullets hurt like hell."

"How would you know?" Brody said.

"Because I've been shot, obviously. It's part of training. Plus now there's paperwork anytime we fire. It's all very serious." She put her arms around his neck and kissed him. "So no funny business. I'd rather not spend tonight in a police station."

One night during college, Brody was at a party. He was with Clarisse. She had her gun on her hip, and the bullets were real now, really real. He'd watched her shoot it once, down at the range. She moved like a well-oiled machine.

So when the big drunk linebacker came out of nowhere and pushed her against the wall and groped beneath her skirt, Clarisse didn't hesitate for a second. Before Brody even moved, Clarisse had kicked the linebacker in the balls, scrambled away, and yelled, "*Stay back!*" as she drew her gun. Just like that, the party went quiet. Just like that, Clarisse was surrounded by armed women. Brody could only stare as the linebacker was escorted away by three women with guns at his back. He was still staring when Clarisse called his name.

"I don't get it," Brody blurted. "You weren't really going to shoot him, were you?

She frowned. "It's not like I wanted—"

"There's no way you were going to shoot him."

"Brody, he attacked—"

"You can't shoot a man over *that*."

Clarisse flinched. Brody shook his head in disgust.

"Men should have guns too, to protect themselves. Then it would be fair."

Clarisse bit her lip, her cheeks flushed red. She rested her hand on her gun. Her hand trembled.

"No," she said quietly, turning away. "It'll never be fair."

THE SIWC STORYTELLER'S AWARD

Angela Post

'Sourdough' was the runner-up in the 2016 Surrey International Writers' Conference Storyteller's Award, judged by Jack Whyte and Diana Gabaldon. **Angela Post** was born in the Yukon and grew up with her Brazilian mother and Latvian father in a mining town inhabited by about 500 people. She writes young adult and children's books when not working as a psychologist. During her lunch-time walks around SFU, the character of the mountain-dwelling prospector, or 'sourdough', began dogging her steps until she wrote about him. You can follow Angela on twitter @angspost.

$\mathcal{S}$OURDOUGH

Hector lived at the very top of the mountain hidden within a thick forest. He hadn't seen a single person in 346 days. He looked around his tiny log cabin. Hector kneeled down by his single bed and pulled up the scratchy blanket to see if there were any cans of food that he might have squirreled away. He pulled out several single, worn, neglected socks caked in years of dust. He went over to the cupboard and opened one, then the other. Only dirt and a few pantry moths flittered around. He sat down on the lone chair. There was one jar, on the rough wooden table that he had built with his own hands from the trees right outside his door. Hector picked up the jar of dried cranberries and shook it. There were just a few stuck to the bottom of the jar. The only remaining nourishment left. He pulled a spoon out of his pocket and dug the cranberries out of the jar. He savoured them as he rolled them around on his tongue. They weren't enough to calm his growling belly. The truth seeped in through the walls of his tiny cabin. He felt it sink into the marrow of his bones. He would have to make the three-hour trek into the village. He would have to replenish his supplies.

Hector laced up his leather hiking boots. Each boot had a hole worn through the toe. He put on his overcoat and a cap that hid his scar. Hector trudged over to the only photo on his wall and took it down. He pulled on the latch in the wall and opened the compartment. He pulled out the wooden box. It had been a very long time. He hadn't looked inside the box since his last visit to town. There had been no need. But now, he counted the coins and stuffed half of them in his pocket.

The trail was so overgrown that he could hardly make out the proper direction. Blackberry bushes and stinging nettles brushed his arms and left scratch marks on his hands. He checked the location of the sun and wondered if he would be able to get to the village and back home again by nightfall. It would be possible to sleep somewhere in the village instead of risking getting caught in the woods at dark. Possible but not preferable. Definitely not preferable.

Hector saw it. The village. A wave of fear engulfed him. Followed by a wave of sadness. The growl in his belly grew loud. With raw determination, he pressed on through the brambles and entered the clearing. He paused to brush himself off. To leave the telltale signs of the forest behind him.

Hector felt in his pocket. No coins. He felt in the other one. Nothing. He thought hard and turned to look behind him. He willed the coins to reappear. Nothing. He looked toward the village. Then he panicked.

He continued on and struggled to come up with a plan. Stealing was a possibility. Or he could offer to help a farmer in exchange for some food. He was strong after all. Able to do a hard day's work. As long as he wasn't asked any questions. He hated folks prying into his business. That's how this whole thing had started. Prying folks. Couldn't keep their wandering questions to themselves.

"Hey, mister. Where you from?"

Hector spun around to see a girl and a boy, maybe about eight years old, each of them. It was the boy that had spoken. He had sage green eyes and sprinkle of freckles across his nose. The girl had deep brown eyes, the kind that could hypnotize an unsuspecting person.

"Just passing through," Hector said, trying to sound as casual as possible.

"To where?" the girl asked.

"None o' yer concern," Hector said, wishing that these two would leave him be.

"You look like you could be lost," the boy said. "Did you need some help finding your way anywhere?"

"Didn't yer folks tell ya not to talk to strangers?" Hector replied, in hopes that they would get the hint and be on their way.

"Nope," the girl said.

"We were told to help strangers," the boy said, "'cause you never know if you might be entertaining an angel."

"Are you an angel, mister?" the girl asked. "You don't look like one, but maybe you are just dressed up like a homeless person, just to test us to see if we can be nice to a stranger."

"Ya, I'm an angel," Hector said. "That's the honest truth." He hoped that this would be enough to send them on their way.

"No way!" the boy said.

"Wow," the girl said, her mouth wide open, gaping at him.

"Mister angel, you have to come home with us and meet our ma and pa. My name is Timothy. But you probably already knew that because you are an angel and you know everything."

"And I am Isabella. I bet you knew that too. We've never met a real live angel before."

"Well now ya have, and ya best be on yer way," Hector said, gesturing them away with his dirt-caked hand.

"You can take off your costume now," Isabella said. "We know that you don't really look that way if you're an angel."

"Where do you hide your wings, Mister angel?" Timothy asked. "That coat doesn't seem big enough to pack wings under."

"I take 'em off," Hector said, growing weary of the questions. He strode away with the two kids trailing behind, hopeful that they would leave once they had their questions answered.

"Whoa! No way!" Timothy said. "Hey, Mister angel, come to our house for lunch. Ma is making stew and she will be surprised that we found an angel in the woods."

"No ..." Hector began.

"You have to come. If you don't, they will never believe it," Isabella pleaded.

"Well ... all right," Hector agreed as he realized that this was an easy ticket to a free meal. He only had to humour these kids and their parents for a short time to get a full belly and be on his way.

"This way. Follow us." Timothy made his way, with Isabella following.

"If you are an angel," started Isabella, "ish that like a fairy godmother? Do you give wishes too?"

Timothy stopped and both kids stared at Hector.

Hector felt the sensation of blood rising to his cheeks, which he had not experienced in a very long time.

"No, I don't give no wishes," he announced.

"That's too bad." Isabella let out a sigh as the twinkle in her eye disappeared entirely.

"That's OK, Mister angel," Timothy said. "I know that angels and fairy godmothers are two totally different kinds of beings. It's not your fault that you can't give people their wishes."

"It's a shame, though," Isabella added.

"We're almost there," Timothy said, rounding a corner and heading down toward an old stone house.

"Ma and pa will be so excited!" Isabella said.

Hector was starting to wonder if he should turn around, when a woman ran out of the stone house.

"Timothy and Isabella!" she scolded with her hands on her hips. "Where have you been? I expected you home almost an hour ago."

"Ma, sorry we're late," Timothy replied, "but we found an angel."

"He's coming to have lunch with us, Ma," Isabella added.

Ma looked Hector up and down, disapproval marking her gaze.

"He doesn't look like an angel," Ma said slowly.

"That's because he's wearing his hobo costume today," Isabella said.

"How do ya do, Miss," Hector managed to get out. He could smell the savoury stew wafting from the open doorway. Hector managed a small bow, trying to look as civilized as possible.

"Your pa wasn't expecting any company," Ma said, "and neither was I."

"Ma, you are supposed to be polite to angels," Timothy whispered to his mom.

Ma frowned and gave Hector another once-over. "Fine. Do you have a name? Gabriel?" she asked with a slight tone of suspicion.

"Hector, ma'am. Pleased to make yer acquaintance."

"Hector." Ma rolled the name around on her tongue. "That sounds familiar."

Hector swallowed hard. He hadn't thought to use a phony name. "Maybe I should be goin'," he said.

"No, come inside for lunch," Ma said. "I insist."

Hector followed the kids' mom, and as they walked through the entrance, a black and white cat dreamily looked up at him. The cat was curled up on a soft blanket by the fireplace. The sun shone through the living room window. The crocheted cover on the sofa reminded Hector of years long past at his grandmother's home. He had spent much of his childhood there. He had sat on his grandmother's lap as a toddler. Hector noticed the photos and paintings adorning the walls. He followed Ma into the kitchen and passed by the well-stocked pantry. There was a full jar of cookies on the kitchen counter with a large bowl of fruit beside it. If only this was his home. Food. Warmth. Family. Things he didn't have anymore.

Pa sat at a large wooden table that looked like it belonged in a medieval castle. "Who's this?" Pa asked.

"The kids brought someone for lunch," Ma replied.

"Mister Hector is an angel, Pa" Isabella exclaimed, tugging on Hector's sleeve to show him off as though he was a huge stuffed animal that she had won at a fair.

"Pleased to meet ya," Hector said, growing tired of the angel charade and wishing that he could just take a bowl of stew and go.

"An angel?" Pa inquired.

Ma plopped a bowl of stew on the table along with two thick slices of freshly baked sourdough bread. "Yes, an angel." She addressed Pa with a wink. "Sit down here, Hector, and have some lunch."

Timothy and Isabella sat across from Hector as he slurped his stew and chewed with his mouth mostly open.

"I guess angels don't have to have manners," Isabella said, dabbing her mouth with her napkin.

"Isabella, don't be rude," Ma scolded.

"It's OK, ma'am" Hector said as he grabbed a napkin.

"Are you from these parts?" Pa asked as he stared at Hector's long beard.

"Just passin' through."

"Where you going to?" Timothy asked.

"Just have to get food and go back to my home," Hector said.

"You need to take food back to heaven?" Isabella asked with wide eyes.

"Sometimes we run out of food there," Hector said, aware that he was walking a tightrope between the kids' expectations and the parents' suspicions.

"We can give you food," Timothy said. "Lots of it! Pa just came back from the village with food."

Pa was silent. He looked over at Ma.

"We could probably arrange to send a few items home with you," Ma said.

"That wouldn't be needed, ma'am," Hector started.

"We insist," Isabella said, running over to the pantry. She read out the labels on the containers. "How about rice, and beans, and dried apricots? Do they need those all in heaven?"

Hector looked over at Pa and Ma. "That would be mighty sweet of ya."

Ma went over and made up a big package of food for Hector. "Timothy, go get a bag to put all this in so that Mister Hector can carry it with him."

"OK, Ma." Timothy disappeared and reappeared with a burlap bag.

Pa slowly formulated his words. "I heard of a man named Hector a few years back. He lost his wife and son when the river flooded. Terrible storm. Horrible tragedy."

Hector swallowed hard, the stew turning to lead in his gut. "That's a sad story, sir."

"That's not exactly lunch conversation." Ma wrinkled her nose at her husband. She put all the items inside and presented the bag to Hector. "We wish you well."

Hector grabbed the burlap sack. "Why thanks, ma'am." He turned to leave.

"Mister angel," Isabella started, "come back and visit us."

Hector paused. "I don't know ... Well ... if ya kids behave yerselves, I just might come back and grant ye a wish."

Hector made his way up the bramble trail. His pack was heavy and the blackberry bushes scraped his skin, but he hardly noticed it this time. Lost in the past. The past that he had tried to push back with all his might. It came in like a monsoon. Pelting him with memories. So many memories. Tiny hands in his. Then gone. A woman to care for that was no more. Hot tears carved their way into his weather-hardened cheeks. Tears that had never come. Hector cried out in agony. The trees witnessed his pain. He found his way to the tiny cabin, exhausted. He fell on his bed.

One lone photo gazed down at him. His wife and young son. Taken away. Stolen from him. He gingerly took down the photo and cradled it as though it was a newborn child. He rubbed at his scar. The angry reminder of how he had tried to save them and failed. He had failed his family.

Something in him let go. Let go of the pain. Let go of the disbelief that it had happened. They were gone, and he would have to go on.

A knock at the door. Hector turned in shock to look, as though he had been sucked through a portal from another land. A knock. No one ever came. No one ever knocked. Here. In the woods. He wiped his eyes with his dirty sleeves and opened the door slowly. Two children. One with freckles. One with soft brown eyes.

"Mister angel," Isabella said, "you forgot to take this with you." She held out a ragged overcoat as if it was a royal robe.

"Yah," Timothy said. "You don't want to be catching a cold."

"How did ya kids get up here?" Hector managed to squeak out.

"We just followed you," Timothy said.

Isabella held out a bouquet of wildflowers. "These are for you, Mister angel."

Hector reached out for the flowers. "Thank ye, little missy."

"You are welcome," Isabella responded in a sing-song voice, swaying back and forth with pride.

"Pa says that he would like it if you come and have lunch with us every Sunday," Timothy announced. "He said that he would like to see an angel at his table regularly."

"Yah, Mister angel," Isabella exclaimed. "We all want you to come back."

"And tomorrow is Sunday," Timothy added, as though he was issuing a royal decree.

Hector stared at the floor. He looked around his cabin. "I don't have nothin' to bring to share with such fine folks."

"Just bring yourself," Isabella said.

"We got to get back home now," Timothy said.

"See you tomorrow, Mister Hector." The two of them waltzed out of his cabin, leaving the door wide open. He watched them skip down toward the trail.

Hector sat on his bed. It was all too much for one day. He looked over at the photo. The heaviness had lifted. Perhaps it was OK to move on. To say goodbye. To go on living.

Hector awoke the next morning. He had an invitation. His presence had been requested. Just maybe he would go. Maybe this would be a new start. He rustled through his drawer of odds and ends to find something he hadn't used in a long time. There had been no need. A comb. He would comb his hair and go to lunch.

§

Register for the 2017 Surrey International Writers' Conference and enter the Storyteller's Award at siwc.ca

25th Annual Surrey International Writers' Conference
Oct. 20-22, 2017

GRUFF

Kris Sayer

Kris Sayer *believes in doing hands-on research, all in the name of her comics. She's created costumes of characters, learned how to ride a horse, practised historical European martial arts, and even travelled to Iceland to study the goats that live there (seriously). Her art frequently features these Icelandic goats, and this comic is all about one of those lovable-frustrating creatures. Have we mentioned she loves goats? Her comics, including the Caprini-based ones, can be read at wealdcomics.com*

You came back!

Pft, not...

...not that I care.

Aah...

AAAH!

AARGH!

ALLAIGNA'S SONG: ARIA

JM Landels

Allaigna's Song: Aria *is the second novel in the Allaigna's Song trilogy by equestrian swordswoman, artist, and editor JM Landels. The first book,* Overture, *was printed serially in issues 1 through 11 of* Pulp Literature, *and is now available in a single volume from Pulp Literature Press.*

PREVIOUSLY IN ALLAIGNA'S SONG ...

Fleeing an unwanted betrothal and enraged by her family's lies concerning her parenthood, fourteen-year-old Allaigna has set off to find her true father. However, her quest is interrupted a mere three days in, when a chance encounter lands her in the illegal poaching encampment of her betrothed-to-be, Tiern Doniver. She is nearly recognized but escapes, thanks to new-found allies: the stable boy, Raddick, and the kennel master, Dog.

Fourteen years ago: Lauresa and her mother Irdaign have been reunited with the birth of Allaigna, but years of separation, anger, and memory loss leave unhealed wounds. Irdaign makes herself a part of the household under the assumed name of Angeley, while Lauresa struggles to forgive her and reconcile herself to her new role as mother. For reasons of her own, Irdaign clandestinely reunites Lauresa with her lover and Allaigna's father, Einavar.

ℐRDAIGN'S CHORUS

He is already at the prescribed rendezvous point, where Clothmarket meets with the New Road. The tavern beside the well is always crowded, though never with castle-folk. Seamstresses, tailors, merchants, cordwainers, glovers, and haberdashers gather here for small ale, fresh water from the fountain, and gossip.

I set my bag, heavy with goods from the apothecary and spice merchant, down between my feet and begin to work the pump handle. It is our prearranged signal and he crosses quickly to the fountain, gallantly taking over the chore of pumping up a bowl of water to wet my mouth.

"Your Highness," he says, proffering the bowl.

"Not anymore," I say sharply, then smile to soften the sting. I drink deeply — it is the best well in town, better even than those within the castle. "Here and now, I am merely Angeley, and you are Einavar."

"It is a better name than my own." His voice is cool and liquid, like the water. Not emotionless, just smooth as the surface of a deep pool hiding jagged rocks beneath. "It's . . . an honour to meet you."

"Oh, we've met before, young man." I flash a merrier, more wicked smile at him, making him start. "One day I may tell you about it. But let's sit, shall we? The beer here is excellent, thanks no doubt to the water."

Once we are equipped with tankards there is an awkward pause through which I wait, allowing him to break it.

"I must thank you, madam, for ..." He clears his throat and a pale purple tinges his cheeks. I feel a surge of fondness for this almost son.

"No," I interrupt. "You must not thank me. Your gratitude would make a procuress of me." I smile again to show I am at least partially teasing.

His return smile flickers, nervous and brief, then disappears again. Oh, how serious and worried he is!

"Einavar," I take his long-fingered hand within my own two. It is strangely smooth for one who has spent so much time ranging. "I love my daughter above all else ——"

It is his turn to interrupt me, his free hand covering our other three.

"As do I. But ..." He swallows, breathes, continues. "Because of that I would not bring dishonour or pain upon her. I ... we ... did not —— "

"Please!" I exclaim, pulling my hands out from his. "Do not tell me what you did or did not last night." The mauve tinge on his cheeks spreads and reddens. "Dishonour is within my skill to prevent. Pain ..." It is my turn to sigh. "She has suffered much already. I would have her gain what joy she can."

His own brow is creased in that same pain. "Wouldn't it be better for her to ... to simply forget me?" The suggestion is agonizing to him, but he offers it nonetheless.

I shake my head. "If she gives her heart to her husband, it will be worse." As I say it, I realize the Sight has returned and settled on my brow. I blink, forcing away the things I hope won't come true.

"Love is a rare and precious commodity, Einavar. Cherish it when it finds you, and never relinquish it."

Another shake of the head brings me back to the present.

"I would not accept your gratitude, but I will accept your troth. Ceilaj bound his to me when I was Princess still. He recommended you to me, and you saved Lauresa's life on the Clearwater Way. More than that." I smile once more. "You've given me a granddaughter any prince would be proud of."

I watch the emotions flicker through his pale, pale eyes: grief, equal to my own, at the mention of Ceilaf; pride nowhere equal to mine at the mention of Allaigna. But that can and will be nurtured.

"I need eyes and ears within Brandishear. For this I can pay you." I've already noticed the thinness of his cloak, the fraying on his sleeves. "I may even still have enough connections to secure you a commission. Rangers, I think? Through indirect channels, of course."

He is about to protest, but I stop him. My plans have no room for false modesty and polite demurrals.

"Meeting here is not safe, though. I will show you a place in the Eastern Forest, and give you a token that will allow you to contact me through a scrying pool there." I can see he is about to protest his ignorance of magic. "It is a simple enough trick. I can teach you.

"And I will, when it can be arranged, show you glimpses of your daughter . . . and mine."

The gratitude hidden beneath those frost grey eyes nearly staggers me, and makes me hope I am not making an error.

LAURESA'S CHORUS

He is gone again, and Lauresa is left raw and aching once more, the wounds she thought healed bleeding freely.

They have agreed it is best for him not to come near too often. But it is impossible for him to never return. He has held the child in his arms and fallen in love with her sweet breath. However cruel it is to Lauresa to have him reappear at sparse intervals in her life, it would be infinitely crueller to deny him precious glimpses of his daughter, who is growing and changing so fast. Whatever her burdens and sorrows, his will be harder to bear.

She doesn't know whether to curse or thank her mother who arranged this meeting. The childish, still-adolescent part of herself is indignant, outraged that her mother has even the knowledge of Einavar, and worse, that she can procure him as if she were a common panderer. And yet, now that it has happened, and the pain of saying goodbye is even worse than the first time, she wouldn't have it any other way.

With her heart reawakened to him, she is more conscious than ever of the cuckoo she has brought to her husband's nest. As Allaigna grows, she looks more and more like her natural father. The child wears a linen cap to cover the straight black hair that is neither Allenis's dark brown curls nor Lauresa's golden ones, and to disguise the Ilvani cast to her ears and forehead. As the years go by and the baby fat falls away from her high-planed cheekbones and delicate limbs, the differences become harder to hide.

So Lauresa takes to hiding the child herself, keeping her away from Allenis's scrutiny when he's at home, which thankfully isn't often. And in trying to protect Allaigna, she makes her a stranger to her supposed father.

VERSE 4
NEW FRIENDS, NEW ENEMIES

As unkempt and ragged as Dog looked, he was fit enough: fitter than Raddick and I, who struggled to keep up as the older man trotted through the ill-lit woods, a hound at each heel. The fall from Nag, the bump I'd given myself on the chin, and Doniver's blow to the face compounded to make me both light-headed and lead-footed. My condition was made worse by the utter lack of sleep and the bone-draining exhaustion of having used so much magic. Finally, after half a bell or so of rough jogging up the ridge and east along the tree line, I fell to my knees, retching but desperate not to vomit.

Raddick stumbled to a stop beside me and called to Dog to halt his steady pace. As I kneeled there, shaking and heaving, I felt a tentative, friendly hand on my back.

"You hurt?" he asked, his voice no more than a pair of gasps.

I shook my head, even though it made the nausea worse, and sat back on my haunches, brushing leaf mould from my hands and knees.

"My horse," I breathed. "I need to get my horse back."

It wasn't just that I was fond of the beast, or that I needed him to carry me over the leagues I planned to travel in search of my true father. It was that he carried too much of me with him. My sword, the one I'd trained for then lost and won again in Rheran; and my bow, the one Rhiadne had given me, that had been fashioned by her father: both these weapons hung from Nag's saddle, along with all my provisions, that cursed pig carcass, and my spare clothing. More important than all these were the little things I'd taken from home, such as one of Mother's thimbles, a pair of herb scissors from Angeley's workshop, a scroll of Ilvani text from the archives that I had only begun to translate, and letters. The letters Mother and Angeley had written to me during my stay in Rheran two years ago; they were the worst. I had been foolish to bring them with me, for they told far too much about who I was. If I retrieved my horse and my belongings, I resolved to burn those missives.

Dog shook his head and made a series of hurried hand gestures accompanied by whistles and clicks. He was mute, I realized at long last, not deaf as the Barrel had claimed, nor the mooncalf I'd taken him to be. Raddick seemed to understand him, though.

Raddick nodded and said to me, "It's too dangerous. Lord Doniver'll be in a killin' mood." That much I understood without translation as Dog slid a finger across his throat.

I shrugged. "You don't have to come." I stood, turned, and began trudging off to the south, toward the forest edge where I hoped I could pick up Nag's tracks by morning. They couldn't be that far off.

After a hundred yards or so, the brush crackled behind me and the hounds caught up, followed by their master and Raddick.

I turned back. "No, really, you don't have to." I was beginning to wonder if this was some subtle play to recapture me. Then I remembered the blow to Doniver's head. That was no ruse.

Dog whistled the hounds to heel and then stood beside me, pointing at my calves. I froze while the pair of them sniffed my feet and lower legs, and flinched as Dog grasped my wrist and held it out, knuckles forward, to the questing canine noses. Of course, my hands were covered in Nag's scent, as were my legs.

Dog made a sound almost like a bark itself and pointed ahead. The hounds surged forwards, muzzles to the ground, tails high, weaving through the woods for a trace of scent.

When we emerged from the woods at last, they sounded. Dog silenced them with another yelp then pointed again, this time in the direction indicated by the turf torn up by Nag's shoes. The questing pair loped away, the rest of us struggling to keep up. The tracks, unfortunately, curled back toward the camp. The beast could not resist the company of the other horses there.

The half-light of dawn was upon us now, and I could see the palisade clearly. The gates were open and a single dog sniffed around outside. My heart dropped into my aching feet. Nag was back in that compound, which to Raddick, Dog, and me was as safe as a bear trap. Across the tussocky field, a third point of the triangle, was the place we'd left Doniver. There was no way to tell from here whether he still lay in the dirt, had risen on his own, or had been carried away.

"I've *got* to get my horse back," I hissed at Raddick, hoping somehow this stable-lad no older than I would have some clever plan for doing so. "And my saddlebags."

"Yer lucky to have yer skin right now," he hissed right back at me. "There's no way you can walk in and back out of there with that, never mind the horse."

Dog made some gestures and clicks, which Raddick seemed to understand.

"We'll get the horse." He nodded agreement at Dog. "Doniver doesn't know who beaned him. Maybe he never will. If anyone has a chance of getting past the other hounds, it's Dog. Maybe they'll be too busy still to notice us or stop us." It sounded as if he was talking himself into it.

If I were an adult, I would never have allowed it. But for all my fierce independence I was still a child of fourteen, used to bowing to the authority of age, at least when uncertain of myself. I was a daughter of nobility, accustomed to having people at my disposal and unused to asking why. It didn't occur to me that that same deference shouldn't extend to the ragged and bloodstained travelling singer I appeared to be. It wasn't till many years later that I fully comprehended why this odd pair decided to align themselves with me, and risk their own necks in doing so. At the time, I accepted their allegiance without question, and without the sense of responsibility that should have gone with it.

§

Stretched belly-down behind a low hedge of rock and gorse, I was hard pressed not to fall asleep as the morning sun crept up behind me and warmed my back. Despite the worry that gnawed at my gut, my exhaustion from the sleepless, terror-filled night was overriding. I didn't drift off entirely, just far enough for my mind to make up strange daydreams. When the sound of hoof beats broke my reverie, they were the stampede sounds of a full cavalry charge. In those in-between seconds Teillai — or was it Rheran? — was stormed by a vanguard of ancient Imperial troops aboard grey chargers.

My eyes snapped open to reveal only Nag, and not two, but a dozen hounds coursing beside him. Raddick and Dog clung to his back. I scrambled to my feet as they skidded to stop. Dog flung himself out of the saddle and offered me a leg up behind Raddick. I wasn't too proud to take it. Dog practically flung me over, and I had barely grasped my arms around Raddick's waist before he kicked Nag forward.

There was a hue and cry from the encampment, the second that day, and two men emerged, hurtling after us on foot.

"The others'll be out soon on horses," Raddick panted, as if in answer to my unvoiced question.

Dog was waving us on, and Raddick turned Nag toward the trees.

It was then I noticed that I was sitting right on the saddle's skirts, behind the cantle. The pig carcass was gone — good riddance — but so were my saddlebags.

"Back!" I screamed at Raddick. "We have to go back!"

Whether he heard me or not I never knew, and Nag continued to thunder on.

*L*AURESA'S CHORUS

Allenis never makes any accusation that Lauresa came to him already pregnant. She almost wishes he would, so she could build a lie and use the stories she's created to defend herself and her cuckoo child. His absolute silence on the matter is unnerving.

Allenis doesn't share the bedchamber she, Allaigna, and Angeley sleep in. He did, during the first months of their marriage, but after the baby's birth he returned to his bachelor rooms and study on the eastern side of the keep. When he is at home, that is.

Tonight, though, he steps into Lauresa's room, softly pulls back the bed curtains and watches as Lauresa finishes nursing the child to sleep.

Lauresa tucks her breast back under her disarranged chemise and pulls the coverlet up to Allaigna's gently rising chest. She starts slightly as she sees Allenis, and puts an admonitory finger to her lips, warning him not to wake her.

He shakes his head. He's had this warning many times. He offers her a hand as she rolls off of the bed and oddly does not let go once she's standing. Puzzled, she follows him as he leads her out of the chamber, wondering what household crisis now needs her attention.

They walk widdershins around the gallery, conversation made impossible by the tumult of evening noise coming from the great hall below.

She has been in his study four, maybe five times in the three years since coming here. Most of their conversations about the castle happen in her study.

There is wine on the sideboard, and a pair of goblets. He pours and hands her one.

"She's beautiful, our daughter," he says, as if he's appraising a mare or a hound. Though perhaps then his voice would be more animated.

He clears his throat, as if to say more, but stops. Lauresa can see colour creep up his throat. With a bolt of realization she discovers his voice is flat, not because he is dispassionate, but because he is nervous, and it melts her heart.

She nods, suddenly shy in front of this stranger of a husband.

"Nearly as beautiful as her mother."

It's not what he was going to say originally, she is sure. Now it is her turn to blush.

He holds forth his chair for her and takes the smaller stool himself.

"I have been ..." The throat clears again. "Less attentive to you than a husband ought."

She's glad she's sitting down as he continues.

"I ... I confess I didn't want this marriage. And I suspect you felt the same. And with cause, perhaps still do. Nonetheless, you have fulfilled your duties as chatelaine and mother beyond my expectations. And if your duties as wife have been small ... that is my fault, not yours."

She is both flattered and wrong-footed by this speech, and dreads what will come next. Although the marriage is, in all practical senses, non-existent, she is happy with that. She manages the juggling balls that keep her secrets and her duties in careful balance, and she is afraid he is about to toss her another one. Can she juggle them all without dropping some?

She feels she should speak, say something to prevent that happening. But even that may send them all flying.

He must see the fear in her eyes, and he takes her hand,

becoming paternal.

"My dear, I'll not ask for my marriage rights tonight. That would be sudden and … unchivalrous.

"But perhaps, since we had no courtship, nor have I been home long enough to be a proper husband, I thought we should simply start by making closer acquaintance."

He raises his goblet, the question lingering in his hazel eyes.

Tentative, terrified, she accepts the invitation and raises her own.

It is the strangest sort of courtship. Allenis is all solicitude and chivalry, which makes Lauresa nervous. Where has his change in disposition toward her come from? She feels as if she is being led into a trap, and thus guards her tongue and feelings more closely than ever. It only seems to make him try that much harder.

He takes meals with her and Allaigna in the small hall, or even in the octagonal room off the guest chamber. He dandles Allaigna on his knee, which fills Lauresa's heart with terror. The girl, though wary of most other adults at that capricious age of two and a half, takes the attention in stride.

Under the loving eyes of two parents and a grandmother-cum-nurse, Allaigna flourishes. It is this, more than the kind attentions, gifts, and sweet words, that opens Lauresa's heart to Allenis. For the first time they feel like a real family, and it brings back the gentle memories of her own childhood in Rheran. Were it not for the sharp sweet bursts of pain she feels when Allaigna's small face turns solemn and inscrutable like her true father's, or when the pupils in her grey eyes shrink to unreadable pinpricks in the pale field of her face, she feels as if she would be entirely happy.

It is a warm, late summer morning when the marriage is reconsummated. Lauresa and Allenis have been taking their breakfasts more and more in the octagonal room, far from the heat and noise of the kitchens. Allaigna, who eats little and unenthusiastically, has already left them for the company of Angeley and her garden of enticing smells, tastes, and textures.

Lauresa is warm already, but still she languors in the heat of the morning sun, never as hot here as it is on Brandishear's arid shores. Allenis has seated himself on the shaded side of the table as usual. Today they linger longer than normal, and the travelling sun now kisses the tops of his dark brown curls. There are more grey hairs than there were at their wedding, she notes, but in the sunshine they glint like silver.

She finds, to her surprise, a fondness in her heart when she looks at the man she accepted only out of duty three years before. And it is with fondness and gratitude that she stands and reaches a hand toward him, aware of the sun glinting off her own hair and the shoulder exposed by the loose fall of her morning dress. He takes the hand, kisses it.

It is not the whisper dry kiss he bestowed the day they met, or the equally absent ones of their betrothal and wedding ceremonies. Nor is it the rough perfunctory embraces of their marriage bed. It is warm, hesitant, and lingering. He doesn't let go, but allows her to lead him out of the small bright room into the cooler depth of the guest chamber. The bed there is made in preparation of a visit from the Duke of Therein tomorrow. Lauresa parts the curtains and slips her body backward between them, leading him like a tame bullock. But the hand that reaches through her hair to clasp the back of her head is anything but tame, and the kiss that lands full on her mouth, parting her lips, is as passionate as any she's felt. With a shock that sends a shiver through her belly, she realizes she is aroused.

She arches her back to curve into him, appalled by her unreined appetite but unable to resist it. What began as an act of fond kindness on her part has become the satiation of desperate need. He is not Einavar. They are as different as midnight and noon. But the need is satisfied, nonetheless.

After that morning, when they hastily straighten the bedclothes of the guest chamber and put their own clothes in order before going their separate ways for the day, Lauresa finds herself tormented by contradictory feelings. One minute she is languorous and content, relishing the still-warming tingle of intimate touch after so long; the next she is aching with bitter guilt and longing for Einavar. It is absurd: she didn't feel any guilt when she and Allenis first shared a bed. But she hadn't enjoyed those early encounters. This time ... This time she can hardly wait till the next opportunity to avail herself of her husband's body. She may long for the cool yet burning touch of Einavar's fingers, the intoxicating scent of his pale smooth skin, and the enigma hidden behind his silver grey eyes. And yet Allenis is, in his coarse but gentle passion, in the weighty strength and maturity of his body, if not equal to her distant lover, enticingly different, and more importantly, closer.

But Allenis is oddly distant after the fact. He sends his page with regrets to the small dining room at dinner that night, and Lauresa doesn't see him at breakfast either. When they are both in attendance at the arrival of the Duke of Therein and his retinue, Allenis barely glances at her. It is as if these last weeks of their relationship have evaporated like the morning mist.

By evening it has aroused her ire. No one treats a princess of Brandishear, even a former one, like a cast-off plaything.

When Allaigna is in bed, and the guests have retired, she strides to Allenis's study and enters without knocking.

He looks up from the pile of parchments scattered on the desk, startled then ... what? Guilty? Annoyed?

"Husband," she says, without waiting for him to speak. "Have I offended you?"

He blinks, a mix of emotions rippling through his reddening face as he stands.

His stammer as he replies annoys her further. *You are the Duke of Teillai*, she thinks with scorn, *not some bumbling country oaf, some unwashed boy. Speak with authority whatever truth or lie you have for me.* But as that thought flashes by she sees some genuine pain cross his face. It doesn't matter the cause, it is enough to soften her mother's heart, if not her newly reborn lover's one.

"My ... my dear wife. What—what possible offense can you have caused me?"

She is struck by how dangerous their questions are. Her daughter, the thing most precious in the world to her, is, by her mere existence, cause for offense.

Lauresa's own tongue trips in the country manner she's just scorned her spouse for.

"I ... I." She grits her teeth, irritated beyond belief at her inability to voice her complaint, realizing she cannot do it without seeming a lovelorn supplicant or a whining cupboard wife. She can't even turn on her heel and flee the awkward and dangerous question without appearing a petulant child. There is no choice but to bare some part of herself. She takes a deep breath.

"Your affections, husband," she says softly, demurely even — anything but strident, she hopes — "seem to ebb and flow like the tide. What heavenly body exerts such pull on them, I wonder?"

He blinks, blushes. Blushes, even! "My lady." He steps from behind the desk, takes both her hands in warm square-fingered ones, but cannot seem to look her in the eyes. "Please ... forgive my inattention. Other affairs ... matters of state ... weigh heavily on me. I meant you no insult."

She extricates one hand and with it gently lifts his chin as if he were a shame-faced child.

"My name is Lauresa, husband. I would that you called me by it."

She leans forward — they are nearly of a height — and plants a delicate kiss upon his lips before pulling away.

"My chamber door is open, for whenever you need to set such weight aside for a time."

She turns to leave, hears him release his breath in half sigh, half groan. She smiles to herself, knowing it will not be long.

Thus the happiest era of her marriage begins, and when her next child is conceived she can truly say he was born, if not of desperate passion, at least of comfortable accord between his parents.

It is a far easier pregnancy than her first. Her mother's body knows this road now, and perhaps, she admits to herself, the absence of Ilvani blood within the child's veins makes it easier as well. Her mother claims half-blood pregnancies are often more difficult, and now she is willing to attest to it personally.

Spring burgeons around her: calves in the meadows, the lower yard littered with downy morsels of infant fowl, spring grass and flowers dressing the dull grey stone and winter-tired fields of Teillai. She is burgeoning herself. Her hair, always thick and golden, is too dense and curly to draw a brush through. She gives up trying to tame it and wears it loose down her back like a maiden's. Her skin is pink and fresh, her belly and breasts round like melons. Allenis finds her so attractive he can barely keep his touch from her; even at state occasions his hand will steal to her belly or to the soft nape of her neck beneath its curtain of pink-gold hair.

Her gravid beauty does not go unnoticed by others, either. The local lords, young and old, pay her court as they never have before. She accepts their gifts and compliments with demure smiles, her hand resting comfortably in her husband's warm grip. She is secure. loved, admired — she could ask for no more.

The spring air is glorious, full of the scents of moist earth, new grass, and blossoms. The sun warms her back; the breeze off the fish pond cools her front. The temperature is ideal, the air clean and fresh, and yet she can hardly breathe. She is gasping; stifled, frozen to the core; burning with indignation, humility, and pain she must not let show.

Allaigna is trotting towards her, something cupped in her tiny hands. At three and a half she has lost so much of the pudginess of babyhood, Lauresa realizes. It is an ache within her, beneath the other, sharper pain she's feeling. Her baby is a baby no longer, and will soon be usurped by another. Lauresa rubs a hand across her belly, pushing back at the insistent kicks, trying hard not to resent the life within her.

I cannot, will not, love it as much as I love her, she insists to herself.

Allaigna has reached her knee, the worried crease between her dark brows breaking Lauresa's heart once more. A pale blue egg lies cupped in her daughter's tiny hands.

"Look what I found, Mama."

Lauresa nestles her own hands around Allaigna's.

"Where was it, love?"

"Under the plum tree." Allaigna looks back over her shoulder at the blossoming plum. She turns back to face her mother, her grey eyes clouded with worry.

"Angeley says eggs that fall out of their nests don't hatch. That ... that the mama birds push them out ..."

Lauresa interrupts the worried tumble of words. "Let me see."

She takes the fragile blue orb into her own hands. It is warm, perhaps from the heat of Allaigna's hands, perhaps from the sun. Or maybe it hasn't been on the ground that long.

"Show me where you found it."

Standing on the spot Allaigna points out, she can just see a nest between the pink and white flowers.

"If I put you on my shoulders, do you think you can reach it?"

They try, but Allaigna's arms are not quite long enough.

The little girl is in tears.

Well, thinks Lauresa, feeling the weight of her seven-month belly, *I hope the branches will hold me.*

"What is this?"

The voice booms up at her just as she is reaching toward the nest. She gives a jerk, nearly dropping the egg.

The mother bird, who has been screeching at her from the neighbouring tree, falls silent.

Lauresa holds her breath, stretching her arm out as far as it will go, feeling the branch creak and groan beneath, then lets the egg fall the few inches into the nest. There is no sound. She has no way to tell if it's the right nest, if the egg is still alive, or if the mother bird will push it out again, but she's done the best she can.

She inches back down the branch as, from below, Allaigna babbles at her father.

"Mama saved the baby bird, 'cuz it felled from the nest, and its mama couldn't get it back, 'n' I couldn't reach it so Mama climbed the tree, so the baby will be born now."

Strong arms reach up and lift Lauresa down from the lower branches, as if she weighed no more than an egg herself, and was just as fragile.

Allenis is frowning. "My dear, is this wise, in your state? What of the child?"

Lauresa's glance falls on the excited, radiant face of her child — the only child she'll ever love — and the tears she has held back all morning burst free. She breaks out of her husband's arms and crouches, wrapping Allaigna to herself, as if to bring her back within her body once more.

Perplexed, Allaigna wipes at the tears with inefficient starfish fingers. "Don't cry, Mama. The baby's home now. Its mama will look after it now."

The serious solace coming from this three-year-old throat is almost enough to make Lauresa laugh. Or it would be if the hurt wasn't blocking the way.

Hiccoughing, she wipes her nose on her shoulder and sends

Allaigna off to play with the new litter of puppies in the kennel, though letting her out of her arms seems the hardest thing she's ever done.

Her husband's hand is on her shoulder, his voice soft and apologetic.

"My dear, I didn't mean to chastise you."

She shakes her head, wipes her nose again, and forces a smile.

"You're quite right, husband. I'm in no shape to be climbing so high."

In that moment she is resolved. She will make no accusation, nor admit to her discovery.

Her knowledge of the letters, hidden so carefully beneath the floorboard of Andreg's study, will remain her secret.

They date from long before their marriage, it is true, and she would have no quarrel with them if the correspondence had stopped then. From the rough, untutored hand it is clear the author is of lower birth—no doubt an unsuitable match for the Duke of Teillai. And it is clear the relationship is old and well established. There are references to a son as well, though it is unclear from the context whether that child is Andreg's or another's. Lauresa supposes she could piece that together with a careful study of the missives, but that is too painful a task, at least for now.

It is also clear that her husband's absences over the past four years have not entirely been spent on the campaign borders or at the capitol. The more she thinks on it, the more resentment grows in her heart. It is true she brought another man's child to the birthing bed, but she has been faithful since the wedding vows were spoken. Her husband, it seems, has not been so restrained.

Anger bubbles up, and she is tempted once more to throw this in his face, along with whatever other objects may come to her raging hand. But she won't. Her pride will not allow her to admit out loud she has been made into a fool. And more, beneath that pride, is caution.

For if accusations of infidelity start flying through the air, that dreaded accusation, the one that could endanger her daughter, may also spread its ugly wings.

So for now, perhaps forever, she will contain her pride, her outrage, her hurt. Even if it means never admitting that she had come to love her husband.

VERSE 5

BARE NECESSITIES

Dog clicked and whistled. The bitch, Edda, came and settled her hoary grey head on his knee, looking upward with pointed eyes while he scratched beneath her collar, around her ears, under her grateful chin. They were a matched set, I thought: Dog with his bristly thatch of mouldering straw for hair and beard, his eyes as kind and soft as Edda's. They both watched the sleek brindled male patrol our rough campsite with his inexhaustible bladder.

It reminded me of mine. I'd put it out of mind all morning

and most of the afternoon, but now that we'd stopped to rest, and the fear coursing through my veins had slowed, it was impossible to ignore.

Raddick and Dog, like the hound, had simply unlaced in front of me and wet the tree trunks. Dog, praise Brandis, had at least turned his back, but Raddick had barely moved away from where we sat. I had to pretend to have a coughing fit to avoid the sight and account for my red face. And now how could I, pretending to be a boy, find any pretext for haring off into the bushes for some privacy.

I untied Nag from the tree and cleared my throat. "I'm just taking him off for more grass." Which was ridiculous, as the patch he was currently grazing was ample.

Raddick appeared about to say as much, but Dog clicked and motioned to him. I led Nag off, grateful for the distraction, not waiting for Raddick's translation.

I stayed a long while away from the others after relieving myself, the numerous developments of the day skirmishing in my head while I tried in vain to quell and sort them. My over-riding worry was over the saddlebags, and the letters. Those stupid letters I should have left at home were now in Tiern Doniver's hands.

Raddick broke through the undergrowth and into my thoughts. He had his ugly, dirt-coloured cloth hat in his hands and was wringing it without mercy.

I looked at him clearly, in daylight, for the first time. He had brown curls that made a matted carpet over his head; wide-set, perpetually astonished brown eyes, at this moment more astonished than usual; a high, broad forehead, bisected top from bottom with a line of dirt from his cap; and no chin to speak of. He was short but, I realized from the down of fuzz on his upper lip, at least as old as I.

He gave the cap another vicious twist as a delicate tide of pink rose up his neck and over his cheeks.

"Dog ... He says ..." He gulped like the perch in the fish trough at feeding time. "I'm really sorry, miss. I didn't know ... I didn't know you're a *girl*."

I wondered how Dog knew. *Probably has a nose to match his name,* I thought bitterly. I drew myself up to my full height, which, surprisingly, was on par with his.

"I don't see how it's any business of yours, but is that a problem?" I asked, once more the daughter of a duchess speaking to a stable hand.

He shook his head miserably. His colour, now bright red, reached his broad and grubby forehead.

"No, miss, I ..." He floundered, no doubt wondering as I did how anything in the last half-day might have differed had he known.

And then I realized he was as embarrassed as I had been about unlacing his breeches beside me. I laughed. It was a bit cruel, but I couldn't resist.

"Don't worry, Raddick," I said. "I didn't look."

I handed him Nag's rope. "Bring him back to the other clearing when he's done here, would you?"

With my saddlebags gone, and Dog and Raddick having left the compound in a hurry, we had no food. But at least my precious sword and bow had still been attached to the saddle when Raddick and Dog had rescued Nag.

I unwrapped and restrung the bow. Fatigue-haunted as I was, sleep was not in the cards yet.

"I'm going hunting," I announced to Dog. "Please keep the hounds close so as not to scare the game."

Really I would have liked one with me, but I doubted they'd leave his side anyway.

The low sun was almost gone behind the hills by the time I returned without so much as a single squirrel or sparrow and nothing more than a handful of winter-dried hawberries.

We chewed the bitter things in silence for a while, until Raddick cleared his throat.

"Miss." Another throat clearing followed this timid address. "Is Nalen your real name?"

"No." I looked him in the eye and lied. "It's Merri. But you can continue to call me Nalen."

"Ah." He nodded, misled comprehension lighting his eyes. I felt terrible about lying to these two, who had been nothing but kind. More than that, they had put themselves directly between me and harm. But with my letters most likely in Tiern Doniver's hands, the fewer who knew my name the better.

"Your saddlebags, I'm real sorry we couldn't get them. Janis had already taken them off——"

I stopped him. "It's all right, Raddick." Another lie, but this one for him. "It doesn't matter, and I am truly grateful."

That last, at least, was true.

It was a miserable night, with only water, berries, and the winter-skinny rabbit Edda caught and deigned to share with us. It was cold as well, and my two blankets had gone the way of the saddlebags. As I shivered myself to sleep, I wished I was brave enough to snuggle up to Raddick, Dog, and their bookends of furry hounds.

Though the loss of the letters proved a more serious problem in the long term, it was of less immediate concern than the loss of my supplies. I hadn't had much food, but what I did have would have lasted me another week or so, and much longer if the wretched pig carcass were still with us. More important was the wooden mazer, and the small open kettle I had been using to cook porridge and heat water. I still had my hunting knife and my father's evil-looking dagger—not that I'd use that to eat or prepare food—but the spoon and the flat metal plate I'd been using as both trencher and skillet would be missed. There were more personal items as well: a bar of Angeley's rosemary-scented soap; my brush and comb; a dandy brush and rag for rubbing down Nag, as well as one or two more feeds of grain; a second pair of breeches, a spare linen shirt; and most embarrassingly, underclothes that were not remotely clean.

After spending some time brooding and sulking over these losses I realized it had only sped up the inevitable. I still had my purse, and we would have to brave a town and do some shopping.

I hadn't set foot in a town since my flight from home. Was it only six days ago? The smartest course of action would have been to send Raddick in with money to buy provisions. Though he risked recognition as a runaway servant, he knew the town better than I and was less likely to set foot in the wrong place. But I didn't trust him that far yet, nor was I about to have him purchase small-clothes for me. The choice of town was difficult too. We were, all of us, wary of Doniver's seat, but it was the only city of size within two days' ride. The smaller surrounding villages, though less likely to contain Tiern Doniver, were also less likely to contain the goods we needed in any quantity or quality, and more likely to have residents who might remember the odd sextet of persons and beasts we comprised. Anonymity was far easier in a populous place.

Like Osthegn in Teillai or the Bastion of Rheran, Doniver's castle, White Tooth, rises above the town, dominating it. The towering central keep for which the castle earned its name is taller than anything on Osthegn or the Bastion, though. A huge cylindrical chimney, it is windowless until at least thirty yards above the ground. Soaring high beyond that, its white stone seems to pierce the sky. It is rumoured the dungeons beneath run as high as the tower is tall. Fortunately I have not yet had occasion to count the downward steps. As Raddick and I entered the lower gates of Doniver with the morning traffic, the White Tooth felt like a sword waiting to fall upon us.

With little sleep, less food, and my head starting to ache from the combination, Raddick and I battled the crowds entering Doniver that day.

"Food last," I said to Raddick, denying the complaint of my own stomach as my companion veered toward the market. "It'll be heaviest, and we don't want to pack it around." As I said it, my belly made dragon-like grumbles, causing me to avoid Raddick's pitiful stare.

"But maybe we should eat something first," I amended, feeling a pang of guilt for Dog, who, with the hounds and Nag, awaited us in a covey well past the commons.

Across the road was a tavern spilling noisy patrons onto the cobbles and sending forth the aroma of stewing meat amidst the beery air. I grabbed Raddick by the elbow and dragged him across the teeming foot and cart traffic to the open door of the Gosling. Such an innocent name belied the tavern's contents.

It was the first time I'd ever been to a drinking house, and I tried not to let my unworldliness show as I peered around the massive shoulders and backs of patrons. There was no place to sit, so we elbowed up to the bar, both of us so short as to barely catch the taverner's attention. Raddick had been making strange embarrassed noises all this time, and finally, as we waited for our bowls of pottage and cups of beer, I asked him what was wrong.

"I haven't any coin," he hissed at me.

"I know that." Was he embarrassed at not being able to gallantly treat me to a meal? "You can pay me back another time," I added, to assuage his pride.

Having to feed two more mouths—four if I counted the dogs—was going to diminish my purse at better than three times the planned rate. Really, I thought, I should abandon both of them. But I couldn't. It was not just because I felt guilty for causing the furore in which they'd lost their employment, and not just because I was in debt for the risk they'd taken on my behalf. It was a little less lonely, a little safer than being on my own. And in a strange way I found I was enjoying the sensation of being able to provide for them. It was, I was shocked to recognize, not unlike the sense of *noblesse oblige* my mother and nurse had fruitlessly tried to instil in me over the years. How ironic to have it surface at last, far from the vassals for whom I was supposed to feel responsible.

As a rule I never touched meat and seldom fowl, but today I gobbled the stew, with its sparse and unidentifiable lumps of brown matter, as if it were pudding. The beer made my headache worse, but I drank it nonetheless, fearing to hazard the water, while Raddick told me a little of himself.

He was from here, or rather Donwych, the village just northeast. His family had been farmers till his father died after being trampled by spooked oxen and dragged by his own plough. It had been a lingering death, and Raddick, though only five at the time, remembered it well. Lord Eiglin, Tiern Doniver's father, had retaken the leasehold, asserting that Raddick's mother and older sister were unable to work the fields. Both of them landed as scullery maids in White Tooth, and Raddick in the poultry pens. When he proved diligent at that he was moved to the kennels, and then to the stables. It didn't seem so bad to me, the way he described it matter-of-factly, but as I thought more it began to bother me.

"But ... your family were tenant farmers?" There were very few serfs in Aerach: serfdom occurred only when a farmer was unable to pay his rents. Even then, the condition was not hereditary. No one could force a family into generational bondage.

"Aye."

"And not in debt? Your rents were paid up when your father died?"

"So Ma told us."

"Then Eiglin Doniver had no right to seize your land!"

I became aware my voice had risen, turning the nearest few heads in the noisy room. I hunched over my beer.

"But with Da gone," Raddick said, "we couldn't work the land."

"Was that proven?"

He looked at me with a blank expression.

"Did they give your mother a chance? To try? To hire hands for the harvest and sowing?"

He scowled defensively. "I dunno. I was only a wee lad."

I leaned across the empty bowls, feeling like the older sister I never was to my own siblings. "Raddick, if they didn't give her the chance to farm it, then the seizure was illegal. Your family could still have the right of leasehold."

He slumped over his beer. "Don't matter," he said. "Ma died two summers back."

There was such a bleak look in those usually soft eyes I didn't press him for details, nor even offer sympathy.

"Chessa," he said, his look even more hopeless, "she wouldn't want to be no farmer. Not now. And me ... after all this" — he waved his hand around, indicating our shared predicament — "it's not like I'll ever get it back from Doniver, will I?"

I dropped my eyes. "I'm sorry, Raddick," I said, then offered words even rarer and more painful for me. "It's all my fault."

"No. No!" He straightened. "I couldn't bear it there at the camp anyway. I woulda left soon — soon as I could figure a way." His face was as twisted as his cap, which was back in his hands and being slowly tortured. "I couldn't do it, keep tending them poor creatures, and sending 'em off to fight to death. I just ... just weren't brave enough to figure a way to stop it. An' here you did it in just one night — " He broke off, giving the cap another violent wrench.

"M'lady." He made a pair of bobbing dips, and I thought he was about to go down on one knee here in the barroom. Fortunately he possessed the discretion, or lacked the courage, to finish the motion. "M'lady, I'd rather pledge myself to your service. If you'd have me, that is."

"Hst! Who says I'm a lady?"

"You do, miss. When ye speak. The things ye know, like."

I couldn't help glancing around the room, though it seemed no one was interested in the conversation of a pair of ragged boys.

"Stop it. Stop calling me that. I'm just ... I've been more fortunate than most. I'm nothing. Nobody." Panic had begun to well up in me. I didn't want him even speculating on my heritage. "And remember: I'm a boy, like you."

This time he looked around the room, then hunched over in so obviously furtive a gesture it was lucky indeed that no one seemed to care about or even notice us.

"Look," he said. "I don't know why you're running away from home."

I hadn't told him that. Was it that obvious? The panic turned to a ball of ice in my gut.

"But you've bought my bread, and I've done you a service. If ye don't want me I understand ... I ... I'd just rather serve a ... a minstrel boy like you than the finest lord in the land."

As much as I was touched, I was worried. I needed to work on my disguise. It was one thing dressing as a common boy, but sounding like a duke's daughter was giving me away. I could alter my voice, that much I knew, and having Raddick around as a model — well, that would make it easier. I had to admit I liked the thought of an extra pair of eyes, hands, ears, and a body at my back.

But in return?

"Look at me, Raddick. What you see is all I have, all I am. I've got no lands, no funds past what's in this purse to support a vassal."

"You've yer voice," he said so softly I barely heard it amid the din of the tavern. "That's worth gold and land and horses and armies right there."

A sudden warmth swept through me, at the compliment. But I wasn't about to let pragmatism be swept aside with pretty words.

"It barely puts a roof over the head for the night and a meal for the day. How many wealthy musicians have you seen?"

"None. But I've never heard any with a voice like yours, either." He was blushing now too, defensive. "But that's not here nor there. Point is, you oughtn't be travelling the country with none to look out for you." I forbore from raising an eyebrow at the thought of this skinny, weaponless boy, no bigger than I, protecting me. "I'm offerin' my service in return for no more than a roof when you have one, and a half-full belly so long as yours is full. You've every right to turn me down, but only if you think I wouldn't be of aid to you."

"I'd be an idiot to turn you down." I was trying for a casual tone, but my voice was rough with unexpected emotion.

I took a long swig of the wretched beer. In return, I thought, I was going to see what could be done about the decade-old injustice that had been done to his family. How, I didn't know.

The more I learned of the Doniver family, the less I liked them and the more I thanked fate for the childish outrage that had caused me to run away from home before the betrothal could proceed any further. If married to Doniver, though, I could probably affect reforms in the land: stop the illegal beast-baiting; maintain widows' rights. If only I could stomach it.

I shook my head, remembering the brutal, ugly look on Tiern Doniver's face. I wouldn't change him, and I couldn't change his policies any more than Mother could change Father's. Was that what she had hoped when she'd agreed to marry him? Or had she simply preferred marriage to a Duke to a pauper's life with my real father? I would not fall into that trap. But those problems were in the future.

*Ir*daign's Chorus

Oh, how I wish *I could take my daughter's pain away, take it as my own, the way I can ease a birth or heal a festering wound. Why is healing the heart beyond my skills?*

Of course I knew of Andreg's lover, have known since . . . Well, I can never remember how long I have known things. It is one of the many reasons I brought Einavar back into Lauresa's life, that knowing. But even still, I haven't been able to prevent or salve the pain.

I have watched helplessly as she tumbled into love with her husband, my attempts to warn or steer her away interpreted as a manifestation of animosity between myself and Andreg. And that, as in any mother-daughter-husband triangle, could serve only to push her faster into Andreg's arms.

"I told you thus" would be worse than useless.

For now, all I can do is love her and feel her pain as if it were my own.

Einavar has not visited her in over a year. Whether he sensed her heart's division, or whether Fate has simply caused his duties with the Brandishear Rangers to keep him away, the effect is the same. Lauresa is doubly bereft, both of her husband, whose lack she had never felt before, and of her lover.

But then I smile and recognize Fate's wisdom, if such a force can be said to have so human a quality. Husbands and lovers are not what she needs, but a mother and daughter. Between the sudden doting attention she bestows on Allaigna, and the motherly care I can wedge around her when she isn't looking, we bookend her, shelter her from the outer world, and remind her that, more than a Duchess, a wife, a lover, she is above all a mother.

Unlike what I feel for Lauresa, I have no aching desire to take away Allaigna's pain. Perhaps it is because there is a gap between our generations — a buffer that allows me to see her with no less love but with less involvement. Nourd told me once that a mother already carries all her babies within her, even before she is born. In that sense then, I carried Allaigna and Allenry and all Lauresa's other offspring within my belly all the while I carried her. It is a surreal yet comforting thought. It is not that my love for my granddaughter is any less; it is simply that I am far enough removed from the type of pain she suffers that I can see it for the transient, necessary, character-shaping anguish it is.

And for all that — maybe because of it — I am able to hold her hand and support her through the first awful trauma of her young life: the birth of her baby brother.

I am happy, delighted, and selfishly joyful to be able to give myself so entirely to her. If there is any thought my motherly attentions should be turned to my own daughter, I realize my gift to her is to assuage her own guilt and allow her to give herself fully to Allenry because Allaigna is taken care of.

Lauresa has matured as well. She is no longer a lost child of nineteen in a strange land, new to the ways of motherhood. She is a seasoned mother, more experienced than I by twice the children, with an easy command over servants and nobles that I, not born to the role, never achieved. I am so very proud.

I feel the tingling *in the back of my skull that tells me someone is trying to reach me. I pick up the heavy basket of plums I've been gathering, push the sweat-stuck bits of hair back under my kerchief, and head indoors to my workshop. Normally cool in the worst of summer, today the muggy hot air has even penetrated this sanctuary. It is like swimming in a cauldron.*

I take down my silver bowl from the high shelf, wipe the dust from it with my plum-stained apron, and fill it with tepid water from the bucket by the hearth. While the water settles I wash my face in the plain stoneware basin and dry it on a clean corner of my apron. Sometimes I'm surprised I have such vanity left.

I clear my mind, gazing into the still water of the silver bowl, opening the back of my brain to the buzzing. I let it percolate through my awareness for a taste, a flavour of the caller. It is not a practitioner of the art, that much is clear, which leaves only one likely candidate.

"Einavar."

The taste comes to me as I breathe on the water, rippling its surfaces. The wavelets fold and crease, reshaping themselves until his face appears in the bowl, reflected in place of mine. It is shiny with sweat, creased with anxiety, and the eyes are dark and troubled.

"Einavar. It's been some time. What's the matter?" I try to sound lighthearted, ignorant of my almost-son's distress.

"Angeley," he croaks, his image wavering. "I must see you ... I'll come to the sally port tonight."

"No. Andreg is home. Stay where you are." I run through my day's schedule, seeing where I can make time. "I'll come to you tonight."

I leave Lauresa to put Allaigna to bed. It is still high summer and the sun sets late, so I must bide my time while the household settles. I let myself out the main gates just before dusk. The castle retainers are used to my comings and goings on various errands, so my departure causes no stir.

I walk downhill to Werrancross gate, where a smithy stands, attached to an ostler's. Here I keep Yannina's second filly, the offspring of a Sandbred stallion I left with my Vanner mare one spring five years ago. The young mare is bay like her mother but swift and delicate like her father and the perfect size for me. I keep her at the ostler's for occasions such as this, when I want to move swiftly without anyone in the castle knowing I've gone further than the town gates.

I don't bother with a saddle, just bridle her and slip onto her comfortable back.

"She may be a bit fractious, mistress," Seddan the ostler reminds me. "She hasn't been run in a good while."

"I'll be sure to let her run, then." I wink at Seddan. "I shall be back tonight, all being well."

The youngster is jittery at first, but as promised, I allow her a gallop across the commons. I've sung a charm that makes us less noticeable. Not invisible by any stretch, but unremarkable, unlikely to draw comment or remembrance.

Night has fallen by the time we reach the edge of Werran Forest, so I sing another charm on my eyes and my mount's to let us see as cats and foxes do. The mare spooks at first, unused to this strange vision, but she responds well to my calming voice, and soon we are proceeding apace through the forest.

I leave her tied with another charm at the foot of the scree slope, and climb up, the noisy shale announcing my arrival. As I reach the top, a dark figure blacks out the moon, offering me a hand up.

We embrace hurriedly. I can see the worry etched between his thin brows.

"It is Chanist," says my son-in-love without preamble or greeting.

My heart stops. Why, after all these years, can thoughts of his safety make my otherwise rational heart trip?

And why hasn't my Sight warned me of this?

But it has, I realize. I simply had not thought the moment would be so soon.

"The tinctures . . . ?"

"Are losing their effectiveness. I am less and less in the capital, and have less access than ever to His Highness."

I look up at him, my eyes sharp. "Why?"

"The mages. And the Princess. They are always at his side."

I pace back and forth, worried and frustrated, then kneel at the shallow spring-fed pool that surfaces on this plateau, the same pool Einavar called me from. It is an ancient spring, steeped in old, deep magic that was here long before Ilmari, or even Ilvani, came to this part of the world. The crystalline waters call me. I wash my face, soaking my eyes in the cold, clear water.

Einavar comes near to see what I am doing, but I hold up a hand. For this I need all my concentration.

The water drops from my face as I bend over the pool, my reflection haloed by the light of the risen moon behind me. I sing to the water, slowing the drops to a rhythmic pulse, turning the air thick and gelid around me.

The wards in and around the Bastion are stronger than ever. I push, forcing each drop of water through the surface, imbued with my will.

I can feel him, distant, but drawn closer. I can smell him. At first it is the familiar odour of leather, smoke, horse sweat; then newer ones of perfume, spices, and something — someone — else. But underneath it is still him.

And yet there is another smell, sharp, burning the back of my nostrils, and sickly sweet at the same time. I recognize the scent of madness. Sound begins to filter through, slowed and garbled by the sticky slow time. He is murmuring, distressed, but I can't hear the words.

Sight remains elusive. I push harder, but find only darkness. It is not the natural darkness of night, or of a windowless room, just black nothingness. And then, like a knife in the brain, is another set of eyes, normally soft and doe-like, burning across my vision.

I slap my hands into the pool, breaking the contact, reeling back, dazzled by flashes of light and careening stars before my eyes.

Einavar is at my side, helping me stand.

"He must come here," I gasp. "At least get him away from the Bastion."
My chest is heaving, breath hard and rough scraping down my throat.

"How?" begins Einavar.

"I will give you a missive. Signed by Vishod. A stop in Teillai on his way to Aleran would not be amiss. And he will come without his court." I grip Einavar's hands. "He still must not know I am here, though. I will have Lauresa administer the treatment."

Einavar frowns, a familiar pain flickering across his face.

"Does she know?"

"That he forfeited her life in exchange for a war? No. He was not himself when he sent her on the Clearwater Way, and she must never know."

"But if he is not himself now . . ."

"He is still himself, but not for long. We will see he keeps himself. You must ride tomorrow. I'll bring the message.

"I'm sorry," I say, looking at the pain in his face. "There will be no time to see her."

I do not add that she is busy with her baby and has little need of him right now. That is a pain he doesn't need, just as she does not need his distraction.

As I ride back to Osthegn a pair of thoughts circle endlessly in my head like battling crows. Gwannyn is a mage. *And,* how did I not know?

§

Allaigna's Song: Aria *will continue in* Pulp Literature *Issue 16, Autumn 2017. The long-awaited prequel,* Allaigna's Song: Overture, *has just been released from Pulp Literature Press and can be found at pulpliterature.com and amazon.com.*

ALLAIGNA'S SONG
OVERTURE

JM LANDELS

THE ARTISTS

S Ross Browne
Cover artist, '*The Huntress*'

Multiple-award-winning artist S Ross Browne has exhibited domestically and internationally in over 70 gallery and museum exhibitions. His work exists in private and public collections including the permanent collection of the Virginia Museum of Fine Arts. As an educator using art therapy he has has taught in hospitals and health centres for a variety of departments from paediatric oncology to geriatric care. He has been an instructor at the Smithsonian Institute and has taught art and design for inner city at at-risk youth in New York and Richmond, Virginia. The painting on this issue comes from his compelling portrait series Self Evident Truths, in which the artist seeks to "examine the possible in the perceived introspections and shared history of [his] subjects in classical pictorial representations using delineations of factual chronicles and imagined mythology." We are thrilled and honoured to have one of these powerful women grace our cover. S Ross Browne can be found at his Richmond, VA, studio and online at srossbrowne.com.

Kris Sayer
Illustrator, 'Gruff'
Kris Sayer is an independent game developer, illustrator, graphic designer and comic warrior. In the rare times she's not drawing, she can be found making (often elaborate) costumes and self-studying swordplay (and spoonplay). She is the artistic-half of Dingo Games, the viking-half of Weald Comics, and a regular contributor to the likes of *Pulp Literature* and *Cloudscape Comics*. Her uncanny, 'spoopy' sequential stories can be found on weald-comics.com. You can also follow her on instagram @kris.sayer.

Mel Anastasiou
In-house illustrator
Mel Anastasiou loves drawing for *Pulp Literature* because she loves the stories she illustrates. She draws in black and white, working from imagination and inspired by details from Renaissance compositions. You can find more illustrations, as well as writing tips and news about her books and novellas at melanastasiou.wordpress.com.

JM Landels
Illustrator, *Allaigna's Song: Aria*
JM Landels studied at the Cartoon Centre in London, UK, under David Lloyd (*V for Vendetta*) and Dougie Braithwaite (*Punisher*). Although she is a perennial doodler, she put down her pencils and brushes after giving birth to three children, but rapidly dusted them off when she realized *Pulp Literature* was going to be an illustrated magazine. She blogs sporadically at jmlandels.stiffbunnies.com.

HALL OF FAME

In November we ran a Kickstarter campaign to help us get started publishing long-form fiction. Thanks to the amazing backers listed below — plus a dozen or so who asked not to be listed — we achieved our goal. *Stella Ryman and the Fairmount Manor Mysteries* was launched to great success in April, and *Allaigna's Song: Overture* should be hitting the shelves at the same time as this issue. Here, in alphabetic order, are our wonderful backers.

74titine

A Bursewicz

a mother of an aspiring writer

Aaron Emmel

Abigail Bruce

ACE BAKER

AJ Odasso

AJS

Alana Krider

Albert Liau

Alberto

Alexandra Daughter

Alexia Adams

Allie Douglas

Amanda Bidnall

Amanda Nixon

Amanda Truscott

Anat Rabkin

Andre Kostur

Andrea Lewis

Andrew W. H. House

Angela Dorsey

Anna

Anthony Pierce

Audrey Hui

BCameron

Bill Hargenrader

Bjarne Hansen

Bob Thurber

Brenda Carre

Britt-Lise Newstead

Bruno

C. L. Murray

Carl Lambein, Jr.

Carol McCauley

Cat Girczyc

Cathryn Udesen Parker

Cathy

CC Humphreys
Celia Lewis
Charity Tahmaseb
Cheri Champagne
Christian Deron
Christine Grimard
CJ Richardson
Daithi McHugh
Dana Tye Rally
Daniel Cowper
Dave Wayne
David Vaughan
Debra Sears
Design in 365 days
Devon Boorman
dl clay
Douglas Shearer
Elise Marquis
Erin Ensor
Eugene Lin
Genevieve Wynand
Gregg Chamberlain
Gregory Boorman
Gregory D. Mele
Guinotte Wise
Guy Windsor
Irena Tippett
Isaac 'Will It Work' Dansicker
Jack Mulcahy
Jane D.

Janet Eastwood
Janet K Smith
Jasmin
Jennifer D. Foster
Jennifer Schaefer
Jennifer Vartiainen
Jeremy M. Gottwig
Jim
Jim Tait
Jo-Ann Terpstra
Joanne Waite
John L
Jon Etter
Judy McCrosky
Kat McNichol
Kate
Kathryn Yelinek
Kathy Tyers Gillin
Keith
Keshav Sapru
Kevin James Harris
Kim Peterson
Kirsten Mah
Kirsty Favell
Kris Sayer
Kristene Perron
KT Wagner
Laura Ambrosiano
Laura Sheana Taylor
Laura Spruston

Leslie Wibberley

Lin and John Richardson

M Docharty

M Landels

Margaret Jameson

Margot Spronk

Marika Purisima

Mary Morris

Mary Thornburg

Matthew Hooton

Melanie Marttila

Mikayla Fawcett

Moutie Wali

Mugthebug

Natascha

Nicki Glave

Paradox Girl

Paul y cod asyn Jarman

Peter Halasz

ProfessorCat

R Bruce MacKeen

Rhea Rose

Rhel ná DecVandé

Richard E Gropp

Robert Pope

Ron Wodaski

Ronda Payne

Roxanne Barbour

S Stopforth

Sandra Vander Schaaf

Sandra Wickham

Sara Harrington

Scott Fitzgerald Gray

Sebastien

Seonaid Andrews

Shades of Vengeance

Shan Wong

Shannon Tilton

Sharon McAuley

Simon Birks

Sir Moose

Spencer

Stacy Pena

Steph Laversin

Steve Fahnestalk

Sue Pieters

Susan Lefeaux

Susann Elliott

Svend Andersen

Sylvia Taylor

TA Smiley

Taylore McManne

Terence Waeland

TG Shepherd

Thomas Ally

Tim McGregor

Torben

Tracey Leacock

Trevor Brick

Tyner Gillies

Valerie Chalker Whitfield
Victor Zorman
Vlad Guzman
Wendee Guthrie
Wendy Christensen
WriteWomanWrite.com
Yolanda Blommers

Thank you!

MARKETPLACE

*B*OOKS

Allaigna's Song: Overture *by JM Landels.* Music, magic, and the shaping of a hero.
pulpliterature.com/allaignas-song-overture

Paperboy: A Dysfunctional Novel *by Bob Thurber.* Photography by Vincent Louis Carrella.
shantiarts.co/uploads/files/thurber_paperboy.html

Stella Ryman and the Fairmount Manor Mysteries *by Mel Anastasiou.* Trapped in a down-at-the-heels care home. You'd be cranky too.
pulpliterature.com/stella-ryman-and-the-fairmount-manor-mysteries

Tatterhood: Unwanted Visitors *by Kris Sayer.* Volume 1 of the graphic novel about a girl, her goat, and her wooden spoon.
tatterhood.com

The Writer's Boon Companion *by Mel Anastasiou.* Thirty Days Towards an Extraordinary Volume.
pulpliterature.com/subscribe/the-bookstore

Dear Geist...

I have been writing and rewriting a creative non-fiction story for about a year. How do I know when the story is ready to send out?

—*Teetering, Gimli MB*

Which is correct, 4:00, four o'clock or 1600 h?
—Floria, Windsor ON

Dear Geist,
In my fiction writing workshop, one person said I should write a lot more about the dad character. Another person said that the dad character is superfluous and I should delete him. Both of these writers are very astute. Help!

—Dave, Red Deer AB

Advice for the Lit-Lorn

Are you a writer?
Do you have a writing question, conundrum, dispute, dilemma, quandary or pickle?

Geist offers free professional advice to writers of fiction, non-fiction and everything in between, straight from Mary Schendlinger (Senior Editor of *Geist* for 25 years) and *Geist* editorial staff.

Send your question to advice@geist.com.

We will reply to all answerable questions, whether or not we post them.

geist.com/lit-lorn

GEIST
FACT · FICTION · NORTH of AMERICA

Bookstores

Book Warehouse
632 W Broadway,
Vancouver, BC
V5Z 1G1
(604) 872-5711
bookwarehouse.ca

The Comicshop
3518 W 4th Ave,
Vancouver, BC
V6R 1N8
(604) 738-8122
thecomicshop.ca

**Myth Hawker
Travelling Bookstore**
Canadian authors • Canadian
content • small and independent press
mythhawker.ca

Phoenix On Bowen
992 Dorman Rd,
Bowen Island, BC
V0N 1G0
(604) 947-2793

People's Co-op Bookstore
1391 Commercial Dr,
Vancouver, BC
V5L 3X5
(604) 253-6442
coopbks@telus.net

Regent Bookstore
5800 University Blvd,
Vancouver, BC
V6T 2E4
(604) 228-1820
regentbookstore.com

**Village Books &
Coffeeshop**
130-12031 First Ave,
Richmond, BC
V7E 3M1
(604) 272-6601
villagebooks@shaw.ca

**White Dwarf/Dead Write
Books**
3715 West 10th Ave,
Vancouver, BC
V6R 2G5
(604) 228-8223
whitedwarf@deadwrite.com

Polar Borealis
Paying market for new Canadian SF&F writers & artists
polarborealis.ca

Room Magazine
Literature, Art, and Feminism since 1975
roommagazine.com

Printing & Publishing

First Choice Books / Victoria Bindery
Book Printing & Binding
Graphic Design · eBooks
Marketing Materials
1-800-957-0561
firstchoicebooks.ca

Wesbrook Bay Publishing
Beverley Boissery, author and publisher
wesbrookbaybooks.com

a paying SFᵃⁿᵈF market for beginning writers
issue 3 out now · free download

polarborealis.ca

Room magazine's CONTEST CALENDAR

FICTION / POETRY
1st Prize: $1000 + publication (*in each genre*)
2nd Prize: $250 + publication (*in each genre*)
Judges: Sigal Samuel (*fiction*)
& Jónína Kirton (*poetry*)
Deadline: July 15, 2017

COVER ART
1st Prize: $500 + publication on a cover of *Room*
Deadline: November 30, 2017

SHORT FORMS
1st Prize: $500 + publication (*two awarded*)
Deadline: January 15, 2018

CREATIVE NON-FICTION
1st Prize: $500 + publication
2nd Prize: $250 + publication
Deadline: March 8, 2018

• •

Entry Fee: $35 CAD ($42 US for International
entries). Entry includes a one-year subscription to
Room. Additional entries $7. For more information,
visit www.roommagazine.com/contests.

![PULP Literature]

our awards for genre-
usting fiction and poetry

he Bumblebee Flash Fiction
Contest

eadline: 15 February

ize: $300

he Magpie Award for Poetry

eadline: 15 April

rst Prize: $500

he Hummingbird Flash Fiction
rize

eadline: 15 June

ize: $300

he Raven Short Story Contest

eadline: 15 October

ize: $300

r more information visit: pulpliterature.com/contests

hort stories, poetry, and
omics you can't put down.

ℬECOME A PATRON OF PULP LITERATURE!

By supporting *Pulp Literature* on Patreon with $2 or more per month, you will be laying the foundation for a secure future for the magazine, as well as ensuring you will never miss an issue! Your subscription includes four big issues of short stories, novellas, poetry, comics and novel excerpts delivered to your door or electronic mailbox each year.

Find us at patreon.com/pulplit
If you prefer to subscribe through our website go to pulpliterature. com/subscribe.

Or you can send a cheque with the form below to:
Subscriptions
Pulp Literature Press
8540 Elsmore Road, Richmond, BC V7C 2AI, Canada

Don't miss an issue!

- ❑ **Send me 2 years (8 issues) at the special rate of $80** (save $40)*
- ❑ **Send me 1 year (4 issues) for $50** (save $10)*
- ❑ **Send me 2 years of digital issues for $30** (save $9.92)
- ❑ **Send me 1 year of digital issues for $17.50** (save $2.47)

Name: _____
Address: _____
City: _____ Prov. / State: _____
Postal code: _____ Country:_____
Email: _____

- ❑ Payment enclosed
- ❑ Bill me
- ❑ New
- ❑ Renewal

Make cheques payable in Canadian funds to S. Pieters. Include email address for digital editions and Paypal billing, or subscribe at www.pulpliterature.com.

*for postage outside Canada add $16 per year in North America or $32 per year overseas.